TALES
OF
GLETHA

THE
GOATLADY

TALES OF GLETHA

THE GOATLADY

PARABLES FROM THE HEART LAND

ROGER ROBBENNOLT

COVER ART & ILLUSTRATIONS
BY
EDWARD HAYS

Forest of Peace Books, Inc.
Easton, KS 66020

TALES OF GLETHA, THE GOATLADY

copyright © 1991, by Roger L. Robbennolt

Library of Congress Catalog Card Number: 91-71004
ISBN: 0-939516-14-4

published by
Forest of Peace Books, Inc.
Route One—Box 248
Easton, Kansas 66020 USA

printed by
Hall Directory, Inc.
Topeka, Kansas 66608

first printing: April 1991

cover art and illustrations by
Edward Hays

For:

Pat, who encouraged
Evelyn, Nicola and Grant, who endured
Christopher Huenke, who found Gletha within me
Theo Holden and Gletha White and all the inhabitants
of Bear Run Township:
Herein mythologized in love.

With Gratitude:

to Bev Shiffer,
who made a manuscript readable

and

to all at Forest of Peace Books
for taking the words of a wandering storyteller
and bringing them alive in print.

TABLE OF CONTENTS

EDITORS' PREFACE

When asked about the origin of these tales, the author told of a young boy who didn't like one of the children's stories Robbennolt was telling during morning worship. Roger asked him what kind of story he would like. The boy's response clicked a switch in Roger's psyche. He thought of Gletha White for the first time in years. The initial tale flooded out— along with a bit of childhood pain. The response to these "autobiographical mythologies," which have been told in concerts throughout the Northwest, has been overwhelming. In the process, Roger has discovered a more deeply authentic part of himself.

In the tradition of J.R.R. Tolkein, Madeleine L'Engle and C.S. Lewis, Roger Robbennolt has fashioned this collection of children's stories for adults. In recounting some of his childhood experiences, Robbennolt has offered a place of refuge where the child within each of us can find healing. On one level these stories function as parables of incarnation where the inner child can sing in chorus with the Holy Child within the Resurrected One so that the lost image is restored. Yet the scope of these tales extends far beyond the healing of the inner child. The sharply honed images weave together a blend of laughter and tears that both amuses and calls forth compassion and a fuller insight into the human condition. They are light-hearted tales, yet they evoke a response of deep and genuine human emotion from which the reader emerges with a sense of affirmation and wholeness. They are stories that glow for us in times of darkness and intensify times of light.

Robbennolt, known to his school and concert audiences as "Storyteller," deftly walks the razor's edge between the oral and the written. The Storyteller's experience of "being spoken through by the Spirit" is gracefully translated to the printed page. He was taught his art by a wonderful black teller of tales called M'Butu who told him: "All of us have a thousand tales deep inside us in a special place—a sacred place. Whenever you share a tale from the deep, you should always light a fire—for you hope that the meaning of your tales will burn themselves into your listeners' hearts." In *Tales of Gletha, the Goatlady* Roger Robbennolt has truly lighted a fire.

A final note about this collection: each tale originally was intended to stand on its own. While they still may be read as individual stories, there is much to be gained by reading *Tales of Gletha* as a whole. We trust that the reader will appreciate that, as it is a *mythic* autobiography, there is not a strict chronology to the tales. We also trust that they have been ordered in a way that is in keeping with the chronology of the Spirit. They have been arranged in three cycles of five tales, each culminating in a Christmas story. Without limiting the world of the individual tales, we found a particular thematic thrust in each cycle. The first revolves around reconciliation and forgiveness, the second around personal transformation and "wholing," and the third cycle deals with breaking through old patterns and blindly accepted ways and birthing into new paradigms of Spirit. Like M'Butu we hope that *Tales of Gletha, the Goatlady* has created a context for meaning to be burned into its readers' hearts.

Prologue

She seemed to float there in the center of the field, a slender figure with hands upraised against the waning red of a cold autumn sunset. The Canadian honkers flew in a low, lazy pattern above her, hymning their passage in a minor key. A shot shattered their song. A goose descended in a tight spiral, grasping the air with a single fanning wing. It settled at her feet. She knelt, tenting the wounded traveler with her strange, soft garments. The other geese circled overhead. A song rose from the kneeling woman, a high, clear counterpoint to the raw notes from the feathered throats.

The scene was shattered once again by a curse from a rifle-bearing man who emerged from the timber's edge: "That damned witchwoman. Always gettin' in the way of what ought to be." He stepped back into the forest.

The red of the sunset deepened. She rose with the great bird in her arms and lifted it slowly skyward. It ascended. The tone of the wild song changed to a paean of praise. As I watched in awe from the field's edge, I thought for a moment that she would join the geese in flight. She simply disappeared.

I trudged from the edge of mystery to the hard reality of a shack in Bear Run Township, northern Minnesota, 1942. The township was an enclave of pulpwood cutters and dirt farmers. Formal life centered around a country store and a one-room school, both of which bore the township's name.

Everybody in Bear Run Township *knew* that Gletha—called the goatlady because of the animals she raised—was a witch.

She never dressed like the other women. They selected their chickenfeed and flour in bags patterned with roses and plaids and paisleys suitable for dresses. Each of the ladies of the neighborhood was identified by the number of sacks it took to make herself a dress. Skinny Minnie Masterson was a two-and-a-half. Most were fours. Then there was my cousin Florrie: she was a seven. This, of course, made it difficult for her to obtain enough sacks of a single print, even though there was a continuous network of exchange in the township.

Gletha, on the other hand, wrapped herself in pieces of soft grey cloth that looked like it had been spun by those giant silver spiders which haunted our chicken coop, making the gathering of eggs a challenge. The cloths could not be identified as specific articles of clothing. Whenever she stood alone in the wind, they streamed out behind her, giving the appearance of flight.

Her coal-black hair was long and soft. The translucent skin of her face seemed suspended on light rather than upon ordinary human bones. Her eyes were pools of benevolent darkness.

Gletha, the goatlady, raised goats for their milk which soothed her husband Pud's ulcer. My Uncle Pud was narcoleptic. He would fall asleep unexpectedly on strange occasions.

Women who could not nurse their babies or who had infants allergic to cows' milk found her an indispensable—though embarrassing—addition to Bear Run Township. It was finally arranged that the goatmilk would be available at Bear Run Store so that mothers and ulcer sufferers could obtain the healing beverage without going to Pud and Gletha's supposedly haunted farmstead.

She was an outcast—except when a child was sick and the doctor couldn't come the seventeen miles from Oak River. Then she'd be called to administer one of the strange potions made from herbs we gathered in summer.

Gletha, the goatlady, was my adoptive mother's maternal aunt. I had been born in a prison where my birth-mother was an inmate. She tried to keep me until I was three. Finally, she dropped me at an orphanage with a battered head and three broken ribs and disappeared. Gletha entered my life the spring when I was eight. I was a scrawny, undersized kid severely beaten by my manic-depressive adoptive father. As the beatings intensified, I acquired a terrible stammer. It was the bane of my existence to be saddled with an aunt—and friend—who was assumed to be a witch. The neighborhood kids teased me: "The moon was full last night. Didn't we spot you riding across it with Gletha on her broomstick?" A born pacifist, I still longed to bloody a nose or two in an effort to halt the hurtful taunting:

> Zoom, zoom,
> Two on a broom—
> When yuh gonna'
> Get to the moon?

My problem was intensified by my impression that, of the whole human race, there was only one person she really liked: **me!** No matter where I went in the great pine forest she would materialize suddenly, silently, the very image of the spirits of the dead she delighted in describing to me.

In her incomprehensible pursuit of my presence, she had taken to mispronouncing my name. It was ever *Rogee*. How I hated that sound—soon appropriated by the denizens of the playground at the one-room country school. The younger poet laureates were endlessly creative:

> Rogee, Rogee,
> Can't lay a hand on me.

The older, earthier sixth-graders shaped bathroom verse in which certain processes of elimination conveniently rhymed with "Rogee." A *sotto voce* chorus of contempt would rise as I headed for the two-seater toilet in the schoolyard:

> Rogee, Rogee,
> He's gonna' take a pee.

Then came the terrible day when my older cousin, Tom, shoved me to the edge of destruction. I had been a reluctant last choice for his softball team. In the final moments of the game I dropped a fly ball, spelling defeat. The ball slipped from my clumsy hands and splashed into the water of the nearby swamp. The white globe floated in stark contrast to the sun-tinged yellow water lily at its side.

Tom walked slowly across the playground toward where I

was cowering at the forest edge. A cruel sneer twisted his face. His words, when they came, slashed away any shaky sense of self-worth that remained hidden within me.

"Roge-e-e-e, you're no damned good. You ain't even a real kid. Your dad didn't have balls enough to have a kid of his own. You're a-DOP-ted!"

He made the final word sound dirtier than any carefully crafted profanity of the sixth-grade boys.

He grabbed the front of my faded flannel shirt and shoved me backwards into the muddy water of the swamp pool. There were cheers from the onlookers.

"The least you can do is throw me the ball, Rog-e-e-e-e!"

I floundered in the water. Reaching the floating object, I grabbed it and heaved it toward the towering, taunting figure. My anger, fear and desperation gave my arm unaccustomed strength. The hurtling, slimy missile slipped through his waiting hands and struck him square on the cheekbone beneath his right eye. He cried out in pain.

He gasped, "If I ever catch you in the woods alone and I got my gun, I'll shoot you dead."

As I struggled toward solid ground, I felt as if my heart had been torn out by the roots. I needed to destroy something in return. I ripped the yellow water lily from its swamp-mooring. As I walked home through the woods, I angrily dismembered the innocent flower, leaving a trail of yellow petals glowing in the setting sun.

At the supper table that night I watched my silent father. He seemed to be on the edge of descending into what my mother always called his "darkness." I had to have an answer to the questions which had nagged at me since the afternoon's confrontation. Trying to sound as casual as possible, I asked, "D-D-Dad, Tom t-told me this afternoon that I was ad-d-dopted. Is that true?"

His face twisted into an angry mask. His body went rigid. He gasped, "Mary, them folks promised they'd never tell. We talked to them all. They promised they'd never tell."

He leaped to his feet and tore the rifle from the rack above his head. "I'm gonna' go down there and kill that blabbing little bastard."

'No, Frank!" screamed my mother.

She grabbed for the rifle. In the scuffle one of them pulled the trigger. The explosion shook the tiny room. A jagged hole appeared in the far wall. I could see the cold stars glimmering in the sky beyond.

The sound seemed to shatter my father's will. He released the gun and sank into his chair. His head fell into his arms on the table. He remained motionless and silent.

The only sound was my mother's sobs as she ran through the door with the rifle. She disappeared into the trees.

I desperately needed a refuge beyond the shack in the timber with my brutal father and frightened mother. Gletha, the outcast, had built a healing home which time-and-again was to save me. I stumbled through the starlight toward her waiting arms.

Aunt Theo & the Whole World

It was the spring of the year when he moved in. It was the spring of the year when he moved into the tarpaper shack across the logged-over clearing from our tarpaper shack in northern Minnesota in 1942. It was the spring of the year when Delius Fenstemacher, age nine, moved into that tarpaper shack. When all the kids in the neighborhood gathered out of curiosity to stare at the new resident, he made his initial challenge: "If anybody calls me Delius Fenstemacher, I'll shove his face in the mud. I'm gonna' be **Dilly Fenn** or know the reason why!"

Since he was huge for his years, ham-fisted, carrying about him the aura of a killer—and since it was the spring of the year and the snow was melting and there was plenty of mud for shoving faces into—we all called him Dilly Fenn.

The following morning we kids gathered in the parking lot of Bear Run Store, waiting for the bell to ring at the nearby one-room school. Dilly Fenn had preceded us. He was standing on a granite outcropping at the edge of the lot, looking for all the world like one of those kings of the Medes and Persians which the sixth-graders were reading about in their history books. We huddled by the weathered store, watching him. He stared back at us—hard, drawing us wordlessly across the intervening space.

In a low, sneering voice he split the onlookers apart: "I've got somethin' special to say to the boys."

The girls dropped back in a semi-circle around us. It

seemed like the whole universe was focused on the rock-lifted figure. Dilly Fenn then flung out the second challenge of his two-day residency: "I'm gonna' lick every boy in the school— one a day—beginning with the sixth-graders."

There was a stunned silence. The girls looked at each other as if shaping a silent lottery concerning the outcome. The boys mostly stared at the frost-filled mud in which they were making aimless designs with their shoetoes.

I felt my gut clutch. I was a scrawny second-grader with a terrible stammer. Always left unchosen in playground games, I was the constant butt of every prank and the center of taunting laughter. I didn't want to fight anybody—let alone King Darius incarnate on the rock before me.

The distant tolling of the school bell caused the scene to rearrange itself. Dilly Fenn leaped from the rock, taking the boys by surprise as he shoved his way through us. He led us toward the tintinnabulation echoing through the heavy pine forest. The girls folded admiringly around him while the boys skulked in the rear.

Aunt Theo met us on the porch of Bear Run School. The complex intermarriage among the pulpwood cutters and the dirt farmers meant that she really was the aunt of half the students and a cousin to most of the rest. All the children simply called her "Aunt Theo."

She was beautiful. She carried about her a certain welcoming softness that belied an interior steel spring. Her tough love healed and shaped. Letters and numbers were disciplined into us in the service of a greater cause: to let us know that beyond Bear Run Township there was a great world with which we'd have to deal. That world at the moment was being shattered by a war. Sometimes we saw her cry silently when word came of the death of a former student. She kept saying that there had to be a way of living beyond the violence and the pain.

On that morning she greeted Dilly Fenn warmly, putting a reassuring arm around his shoulders as she assigned him a desk. She seemed unaware that she was embracing an enemy in our midst.

Children of all ages clustered in the single room. The youngest was five-year-old Taddy Thompson. "Taddy" was short for "Tadpole." That was what his daddy always called him. (Seeing him years later, he was still called Taddy. I doubt that most folks ever really knew what his rightful name was.)

The oldest student was sixteen-year-old Pauline Pucharski. She was a newcomer from Poland and didn't speak much English. She didn't have to. All she had to do was walk to the front of the classroom. In the process she raised hard-eyed envy in the girls and certain as-yet-unidentifiable feelings in the boys. She was so beautiful with her golden braids and the sun glinting off the gemstone she always wore on the black ribbon at her throat—a gift, she said, from her "left-behind grandmamma." We kids always called it the Polish opal. We weren't quite sure what an opal was, but that's what we called it anyway. Pauline was living proof that there were great distances beyond our little world. She was also better at geography than the rest of us.

The visual center of our schoolroom lives was the great globe—Aunt Theo's prize possession. It was held in place by wide golden bands topped with the heads of golden dolphins. It sat on a shelf—specially built by her husband, our "Uncle Harry"—just beyond the reach of most of us. If we ever wanted to find a special place—and our hands were clean— the globe would be set gently and reverently on the table. We would revolve it with a sense of wonder and, on occasion, sur- reptitiously stroke the dolphins' heads. The globe was always down for geography time. It was usually Pauline Pucharski who was able to walk to the front of the classroom and point out the most exotic of places, like the Malay Archipelago.

In a rear corner of the classroom stood a huge round- topped stove. It had a second function beyond the usual overheating of the occupants. We were all poor. The school received government issue food: powdered milk and soybean meal. Each day, one of us was given a morning assignment. That boy or girl would take a bucket, fill it with water from the schoolyard pump, mix the milk and meal in it and set it on the hot stove. By lunchtime we'd have a terrible-tasting concoction—but we were often hungry enough to savor it. We could also bring potatoes to school in small, tin Karo Syrup pails. We would place them on the stove, and by mealtime we could leaven our diet with a baked potato.

The hot stove also underscored another feature of the classroom: the smells of young bodies between Saturday night baths. Since it was the spring of the year, the stove's heat accented the aroma of that general remedy for "change of the weather" diseases: asafoetida. It was an odorous gum resin made from Asiatic plants of the parsley family and worn around our necks in small cloth bags. As the room heated up, the garlic-like odor was overwhelming. Its chief strength seemed to be that it smelled so bad nobody would get close enough to anybody else to catch anything.

Not even asafoetida could deter Dilly Fenn. He was true to his malicious plan. He'd hide in the woods. As the chosen victim left school, Dilly would stalk him toward home. If his prey traveled in a group for safety, Dilly would wait until he had to go into the woods to cut some firewood. Then he'd attack. After the beating, the boy became a part of his special corps willing to do anything he requested. The progression of bruised faces and intimidated boys moved from sixth—to fifth—to fourth—to third—to second grade. I was the only boy in second grade. Dilly Fenn, sensing my timidity, passed by my desk for days before the impending event, pausing to whisper, "You'll soon get your turn."

The day for "my turn" arrived. It seems like yesterday. It was a Tuesday. I awoke in a cold sweat. Waves of nausea broke over me as I remembered what I faced. My father came over to my bed from which I should have arisen a half-hour earlier. He was on a slide into his darkness. The violence of his temper would flare into physical abuse.

"All right, you lazy kid. Git out of there."

"I c-c-can't g-go to school t-today, Dad. I'm terrible sick."

"You git yer butt out of that bed and down that hill to school—and it's no breakfast for you."

Caught between my father and Dilly Fenn, I chose the latter. As I went out the door, my mother handed me a small Karo Syrup pail containing a potato. She wanted to hug me as I left—to whisper her sorrow that my daddy's mind was sick—but he stood between us. He grabbed me by the shoulder and propelled me through the door and down the hill.

I was dawdling along the wooded slope toward the school,

considering the possibility of running away—somewhere—anywhere—to escape both Dilly Fenn and my angry father. I heard the sound of ma-a-a-ing coming from a deserted farmstead off to my left. There was a tumble-down shack, a pole barn and a fenced yard. Rumors had been flying about for weeks that, along with my Uncle Pud, she was coming back to Bear Run Township: Gletha, the goatlady.

I didn't much care that she was a witch. Maybe she could provide me with some kind of spell to make me invisible after school and thus evade Dilly Fenn.

I stepped into the clearing, almost falling over a sleeping form seated on a rotting stump in the sunlight, deep-toned snores shaking his nostrils. Nearby, a strangely clad figure was unloading an incredible number of goats from a battered truck. They were leaping playfully around the enclosure, celebrating their freedom. For a moment I wished I were a goat. Gletha looked at me from pools of darkness. That first look drew me to her.

She spoke in a voice of surprising richness: "You must be Rogee."

The hair rose on the back of my neck. I instantaneously hated the appellation. I replied in some heat: "D-d-don't you ever call me that n-name again. I hate it. D-don't you ever call me nothin' but Roger."

"Well, if you hate the name so bad, I'll always call you by it. If you can bear with grace the things you hate, nothing will ever destroy you."

"The only thing likely to destroy me is Dilly Fenn." All at once it seemed right to let my whole life tumble out into the embrace of the tall woman who stood with her arms extended slightly toward me. I ended with, "Gletha, I'll tell you what. Let me stay here with you. I don't need to go to no school. I can help with the goats. I milk cows good. No reason I can't milk a goat. I could hide in the goatshed, and Dilly Fenn and my daddy neither one would know where to look for me."

She kept her silence for a moment. Then she spoke: "You've got to go and learn so that you can get away from all this even when you're in the middle of it. Now, you git down that hill, boy."

For the second time that morning I was propelled down the

hill: the first, at the end of my father's angry arm—the second, urged on by a voice with the power of an Egyptian priestess. As I was about to enter the woods, I turned and asked, "If Dilly Fenn finds me after school and bruises me all over, will you be here to make me feel better somehow?"

"I'll be with you in a special way. You won't feel alone."

"Well, I hope if you're with me one way or another that you're a better fighter than he is."

I continued down the forested slope toward the school. The last echoes of the bell were reverberating through the frosty air. As I approached the building, Aunt Theo was standing on the porch, seeming to await me. She smiled and said, "Good morning, Roger. Today's the day."

I was horrified. She somehow knew that this very Tuesday was the day Dilly Fenn was going to destroy me, and all she was doing was standing on the porch smiling about it. Then she continued as she handed me the empty pail, "Today's the day for you to pump the water for the soup."

I was relieved. She didn't really know and approve of his impending act of carnage. I pumped the pail full of water. I carried it with great care up the front steps, not spilling a single drop. I stepped into the classroom. I was concentrating so hard on the water that I did not see Dilly Fenn. He stuck out his foot. I tripped and went flat on my face, the bucket of water spilling over me. The schoolroom exploded with raucous laughter, underscored by a little chant which the girls repeated:

Clumsy Rog, clumsy Rog,
Doesn't even know to dodge!

At that moment I knew that I had to get Dilly Fenn—and get him first!

My opportunity came at noon. I was handed my syrup pail only to discover that my mother had given me the largest potato I'd ever seen. I laid it on the desk to cool. I looked across the classroom. Dilly Fenn was dipping Pauline Pucharski's golden braids in the inkwell on his desk while she concentrated on the strange English words in a first grade reading book. I caught his eye and stared as menacingly as I could. He stuck out his tongue, gave me a Bronx cheer and went back to his heinous crime.

I picked up the cooked potato and took careful aim at Dilly Fenn's head. I threw it with all my might.

My aim was no better then than it is now. The potato missed Dilly Fenn. It struck Aunt Theo's globe—right on the equator. The globe plummeted from the shelf and struck the floor with a sickening thud. It shuddered into two halves as the heads of the golden dolphins spun crazily on the well-worn wood.

There was silence in the classroom, the kind of silence you might expect if someone stood up and swore in church. Aunt Theo's quiet, steel-edged voice sliced through the breathless pause: "Roger and Delius: walk to the front of the classroom."

Dilly Fenn and I walked nervously to the front of the room.

"Roger and Delius, pick up the halves of the world."

Dilly Fenn and I each picked up a half of the world.

"Roger and Delius, hold the halves of the world together."

Dilly Fenn and I held the halves of the world together, our fingers touching whether we wanted them to or not.

"Pauline Pucharski, walk to the front of the classroom."

Pauline Pucharski, her ink-stained braids marring the perfect whiteness of her blouse, walked to the front of the classroom. The afternoon sun glinted from the Polish opal at her throat. The unsteady globe nearly plunged a second time.

"Pauline Pucharski, point to the Malay Archipelago."

Without hesitation she pointed to those distant islands of all our dreams.

For weeks after that, whenever anyone wanted to find a special place, Aunt Theo would call Dilly Fenn and me to the front of the classroom in order that we might pick up the halves of the world and hold them together—our fingers touching whether we wanted them to or not.

Somehow, Gletha had kept her promise. Something had certainly been with me in a special way. From that day on Dilly Fenn never picked another fight with me. He once said as we roamed the magic, sunlit woods, "Rog, I don't care that you talk funny. I'm going to be your friend for life."

I have always had this fantasy: all the leaders of the world gather in Aunt Theo's school. From behind them comes her firm voice commanding two of them to walk to the front of the room, pick up the two halves of the world and hold them together, their fingers touching whether they wanted them to or not.

If that had happened, perhaps ten years later I would not have found myself standing in the midst of a marching band, playing martial music on my clarinet. Former schoolmates a year or two older than I boarded a train for boot camp. They would later face combat in Korea.

Dilly Fenn, my friend for life, never returned alive from that war. I wished Gletha might have been somehow with him. Maybe she was.

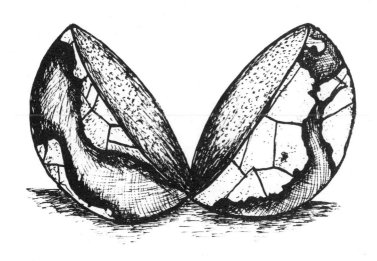

The Fawn

The silence, scored only by the humming of insects, was shattered by the crack of a deer rifle. The grazing buck's head snapped up as if he were a gigantic puppet. Then he folded in upon himself and sank to the ground in slow motion. The doe and tiny fawn paused for a moment—then bolted from the clearing west toward Old Lady Slough as a second shot rang out.

I remained huddled in the hazelnut bushes where I had watched the wild trio live out a pattern of caring. The great buck had nuzzled the fawn as it nursed, contradicting my father's statement: "They sire 'em and leave 'em." The doe had stood patiently while the less patient fawn butted her udder in its enthusiasm for milk.

In the harsh light of a late-spring afternoon, I could see the cloud of flies descend on the poached animal. I didn't dare move. I remembered tales that could not be true—but in my young mind might be—of those who killed deer out-of-season, brutalizing observers into silence.

There was a crashing in the leftover cuttings from the winter logging on the far side of the clearing. The image of its source hit my mind before the person could be seen. It had to be Clint Dunker. The Dunkers and their eight kids lived in a tarpaper shack two miles beyond Old Lady Slough. Clint was an enormous man. He was always garbed in a heavy red and black plaid shirt and wool army pants, even in the hottest weather. His belly ever obscured his belt. His scraggly beard, tiny eyes and wide mouth with a center tooth missing completed what, to me, was a terrorizing mask that was on occasion the substance of my worst nightmares.

Clint never had a dime to his name, yet he always seemed able to join the drinking bouts at the crossroads bar two or three times a week. It was at one such contest that my drunken cousin, Ned, had knocked out Clint's tooth. Clint promised to "finish Ned off" if he ever caught him alone in the woods. With these images flickering on my mind-screen, I remained very quiet as Clint stepped into the clearing. He looked every inch an out-of-costume Viking pillager borrowed from my comic books.

He stood over the fallen buck, gun slung carelessly across his shoulder, his free hand massaging his groin. He was joined by his two oldest sons, near-clones of their father in appearance and action. The picture through the hazelnut branches had changed from one of rare beauty to one of absolute despair. The power controlling life in the forest had turned dark.

"Hey, Pa, d'ja s'pose ya hit the doe too?" queried Pete, the younger of the sons.

"I dunno'. That shot was just for kicks. There'll be enough meat for awhile in this'n. We'll gut him here and let the wolves take care of the evidence. Tick, you tie the rope on 'im. We'll sling 'im on a pole and carry 'im instead of dragging 'im so the game wardens won't find our trail."

The gutting was quickly accomplished. Then Tick, so-called because of the muscle that ever-flickered at his left eye, followed his father's orders. The procession left the clearing in silent triumph.

I scrambled from the thicket and ran toward the spot where the doe and the fawn had disappeared. A clear trail of blood led to the west. A few hundred yards beyond the clearing, the doe lay shuddering out the final moments of her life on the bank of Old Lady Slough. I walked helplessly to her. She turned her eyes toward me. There seemed to be a silent command in them. I was to somehow heal a dimension of the disaster in the woodland family. She struggled one last time to stretch toward the slough. Then she lay quiet in her pool of blood. The cloud of flies arrived on cue.

I heard a faint sound. About six yards from the shore the fawn was struggling. It was up to its belly in the thick ooze. The tales of Old Lady Slough were unending. If you ever wanted to get rid of anything, you threw it in Old Lady Slough. Whenever anyone disappeared and foul play was suspected, there was always the possibility of evidence eliminated in Old Lady Slough where the object would be slowly sucked beneath the surface. Far out in the center of the slough loons lazed on the open water. Their strange calls sounded like the spirits of whatever had disappeared along the shore.

I was in despair. There was no way I could trust myself to the treacherous surface to rescue the fawn. Yet it violated every fiber of my being to triple the tragedy carelessly begun by Clint Dunker. There was only one solution. I would fetch Gletha. I always approached her with a healthy combination of fear and fascination. If ever I needed magic to move an object through the air, it was now—if the helpless fawn was to be rescued.

I ran through the forest, following a fire trail which gave me the freedom of speed. I prayed that she would be at her shack. As I approached, I heard the bleating of the goats. My hopes leapt when I heard her singing the strange, wordless song she always sang as she milked them. "Relaxes 'em. They give more," was her only comment when I had asked her once why she sang.

As I burst into the clearing, she was coaxing her favorite, Old Tilly, up on a high stump. This was Gletha's milking platform.

"G-G-Gletha, you've got to stop and c-come with me. Clint D-D-Dunker poached a buck and killed the doe and the fawn is stuck in Old Lady Slough and you've got to come and help me get it out!"

My run-on shout scattered the animals. Old Tilly kicked over a half-filled bucket of milk as she escaped from the rush of the shrill sound. Gletha, still in the trance of her milking song, turned and stared at me. I half-expected her to strike me or deliver a stinging reproach—the kind of response to my enthusiasm which usually came from my father. Instead, she turned and moved toward the forest edge in the direction from which I had come. Her grey draperies floated in the evening breezes. I was exhausted from the two-mile run. She seemed to be moving with incredible speed.

"Gletha, wait for me!" I gasped.

She paused and flicked a length of soft grey cloth around my shoulders. My body was moving quickly, maintaining an eerie lightness. Her ballooning garments appeared to carry us through the evening shadows. I could almost believe the whispered stories. Folk kept saying they saw her floating across the face of the harvest moon on August evenings.

We arrived at the edge of Old Lady Slough. The doe's body remained untouched. In the distance wolves had already begun to gorge themselves on the buck's remains. Gletha watched them for a moment. The animals paused in their activity, turned in our direction and sniffed, then returned contentedly to their task.

"My babies know I'm here," Gletha whispered.

I shuddered. I had seen her babies, the wolves, tear one of our sheep apart. There was no way for me to muster the same kind of affection for them—or the ability to communicate with them—which she had.

She turned her attention to the fawn. It had sunk into the slough up to its neck. The panicked eyes stared in our direction. There seemed to be no hope of removing the tiny beast. It still thrashed its head, slowly driving itself to the edge of death. Gletha began one of her wordless songs—at least the words did not register with me. She stared in the fawn's direction. Their eyes met. In that instant it stopped struggling.

She began to unwrap some of the seemingly endless pieces of cloth in which she was garbed.

"Rogee, spread these out ahead of you and crawl out to the fawn on them."

I didn't know if it was her use of that detested name or naked fear that made me reluctant. "G-G-Gletha, you know I'll sink. I want to save the fawn—but I don't want to find myself up to *my* neck in the muck as well."

She caught my eyes with hers. A melody shaped itself on her lips. I felt warm and light as if I could float to the tip of the tall pine on the little island in the swamp and join the evening star which had begun to glow there. I did as she told me.

The surface of the slough held firm beneath the film of the strange cloth. I crawled slowly, lightly, toward the trapped fawn. As I came close to the fawn, Gletha said, "Slip your hands down its sides to its belly. Lift slow-like."

The tiny animal was motionless. I lifted slowly. I felt its breath quicken. In a moment its body was released. It rested, mud-covered, in my arms. I crawled awkwardly back across the cloth path. Gletha swaddled the fawn in more of her body-warmed drapes. I crawled out one last time to gather the magic swatches of grey from the surface of the slough.

When I reached the shore, the lightness left me, and I was overcome by a sense of overwhelming weariness. Gletha cradled the little beast in her arms. We moved homeward slowly through the darkening woods. It was as if she needed time to renew the fawn within the circle of her concern.

As we arrived at the clearing, we were greeted by the high-pitched bleat of Old Tilly: unmilked and uncomfortable. She automatically stepped up on the milking stump as Gletha approached.

"Fetch my stool, Rogee."

I placed her low, three-legged stool by the stump. Gletha sat gently upon it. She placed a burgeoning teat between the lips of the exhausted little animal. She crooned a song to the fawn in her arms and the goat on the stump. Old Tilly turned and began to lick the mud-matted ears of her adopted baby.

The full moon flooded the clearing. Through the open window of the shack came the snores of my Uncle Pud, who seemed ever in bed. The remaining goats grazed quietly in the distance. The bearded Tilly, Gletha and the fawn looked, in the shifting shadows, like the Holy Family from a dime-store Christmas card. In the distance Gletha's other "babies" howled contentedly.

In the clearing of my mind shifted patterns of three: the deer family, the marauding men and the statue-like image of love in the moonlight. I felt hope again.

Bread Pudding

"Gletha, I don't want you b-b-bringin' her along—no way!"

"But Rogee, she's lonesome and she ain't got no father around and her mother's a little queer and she likes you."

"That's no cause to completely ruin bread pudding day, and if you keep calling me that d-d-dumb name, I'm gonna' leave you right here to finish all the work."

Gletha and I were grubbing around in the half-dry mud of the hog yard, picking up corncobs. We would spread them on the grass beyond the fence to finish drying in the hot August sun. Later they would be carried by the bushel-basketful to the farmhouse kitchen to be burned in the cast-iron cookstove for bread baking.

My childhood calendar contained no Mondays. The second day of the week was ever "bread pudding" day. My mother baked fresh loaves. At the same time, stale bread from the week before was transformed into Bear Run Township's most famous delicacy. Late in the afternoon the heavy odor of cinnamon would float through the forest, and, as if by magic, shadows would appear at the edge of the clearing to materialize into hungry people the moment the special green baking dish emerged from the oven.

I knew that Gletha would bring her—my cousin, Stella. Stella's mother, Mamie, was the subject of a great deal of neighborhood gossip: "She's feeble-minded" or "That woman's just plain crazy" or "No tellin' who's the father of that odd little girl o' her'n."

I just couldn't stand Stella. I was nine, and she liked me. Whenever I was playing in the woods, I was liable to hear a "crunch, crunch." I'd whirl around and there she'd be: almost breathing down my neck and crunching in my ear. She always wore washed-out frocks and dirty little aprons—and the big front pocket of the apron was always wet and slimy. Stella had a passion for raw potatoes. Before she went anywhere she chopped up a bunch of potatoes, skins and all, and filled her pocket. The sound of her over-large front teeth knifing through the crisp vegetable always caused my own teeth to vibrate. There was also the stare from the great Kewpie Doll eyes—and the slow-spreading grin of triumph: "I found you, Rogee. Ain't no way you can hide from me. I can find you anywhere in the woods. Gletha said if I thought of you hard enough I could always find you. Now will you play with me?"

"D-D-Dammit all, Stella. When are you a'gonna' learn not to sneak up on a guy? Now, git outta' here."

Her response was always painfully slow, delivered in a toneless voice—and always the same: "I'll—tell—your—dad—you—cussed—at—me—and—he'll—blister—your—butt. You'd—better—play—with—me." The smile would harden and the eyes would glitter with malice.

She knew she'd won some moments of my attention—as well as my deepening hatred.

And now Gletha, whom I thought really cared for me, was going to ruin the best time of my week: bread pudding afternoon! She was going to bring Stella the next time the incense from my mother's kitchen overcame the very smell of the spruce trees themselves.

Baking day arrived. The wondrous odor spread on the soft summer wind. The crackling of dry twigs signaled the arrival of "the relatives." I knew who was coming by the sounds in the forest. The slow dragging through the dry twigs could only be Uncle Babe with his polio-shattered leg. Strange sentences sighed aloud heralded the arrival of Uncle George who thought he was Jesus. Today I could make out one phrase repeated over and over again: "I'm going up to Jerusalem for the last time." Then, as if an angry stag were ripping up the brush, Uncle Guy roared into the clearing. His lungs had been "touched by mustard gas" during the war to end all wars. He'd never worked a day afterwards—but he could eat more than anyone I'd ever known. At one country church contest he'd eaten thirty-seven ten-inch pancakes—and then the cooks ran out of batter. The slowest pace of all belonged to sleepy Uncle Pud, Gletha's husband. As I played in the woods, I would sometimes fall over him napping on a stump in a sunspot.

I heaved a sigh of relief that only the men had come. It was premature. On the opposite side of the clearing three figures garbed in shapeless draperies appeared. They looked for all the world like bedraggled Greek goddesses from my reading book. Grandly centered, Gletha had draped the ends of her spider-spun fabric over the shoulders of Mamie on her left and Stella on her right. In the sun's bright glare, the three appeared to be floating above the moss and evergreen cones on the forest floor. Folks said that through witchcraft Gletha could make anything move where she wanted. Watching that storybook entrance made a believer of me.

Stella arrived crunching and grinning, knowing she was the last person I wanted to see. The wheels of my mind turned quickly. Perhaps there *was* a way of enjoying the bread pudding without her oppressive presence. The grownups always sat for a time on the porch, letting the kitchen incense penetrate deeply. Stella would drag me off to the barn to play with the kittens or to concoct some mindless game.

Today I took the initiative. I glued a smile on my face and raced toward her. "Hi, Stella. W-w-wanna' play?"

She looked at me in dumb amazement. She never laughed at my stammer. Maybe so many hurtful comments were made about her that it made her sensitive to the pain of others. It was the first time ever that I'd asked her to play with me. She thrust a potato-sticky hand in mine. I drew her off into the woods. Nobody noticed our quick exit.

I lured her far into the thick-standing trees by my promise of entertainment. She kept asking, "What are we gonna' play, Rog?"

"You j-j-just wait and see. It'll be the m-most fun you've ever had."

We reached a particularly heavy cluster of pine. The rays of the late afternoon sun did not reach the eerie daylit darkness.

"Okay, Stella, w-w-we're gonna' p-p-play cowboys and Indians. You can be the cowboy and I'll be the Indian and I'll capture you."

Her face broke into a beatific smile at the mere mention that I might capture her. She took off running. I pursued her, syncopating a high-pitched yell by pummeling my mouth with my hand. I caught her quickly, and she giggled as I dragged her toward a sapling in the middle of a small clearing. I thrust my free hand into the pocket of my bib overalls which was always filled with odds and ends. I pulled out two long pieces of binder twine, quickly tying her wrists together, then tying them to the tree. I performed the same maneuver on her ankles. I lastly removed my enormous red and white bandanna from another pocket and stuffed it in her mouth.

Stella never protested. She kept looking at me adoringly with her water-spaniel eyes, still overcome by the fact that I had offered to play with her.

I announced dramatically, without a sign of a stammer: "You, O woman, are my prisoner. But I cannot be bothered with you as I move into great battle. I leave you thusly to die in the forest." It may not have been the authentic cadences of the Red Man, but Stella appeared to be proud of my oration.

I turned and ran away toward home as fast as my feet would carry me. I had solved my problem. My feast was not to be fouled by the detested presence of Stella.

I panted my way up on the porch just as the adults filed into the living room where my mother had spread a little lunch on the table (my favorite fish—pickled bullheads—dried venison, fresh-canned peaches, warm bread, blueberry jam and Kool-Aid). It was at this point, had she been there, that Stella was always taken to the kitchen by the hostess. Opening the icebox door, Mother would chisel off a large piece of lake ice for Stella to suck so that we could all have a bit of relief from her crunching. (I dreamed one night that she got a piece with a frog frozen in it—but my dream was never realized.)

When everyone was seated around the table, George insisted that we all join hands for prayer. I reached across Stella's empty chair and took Gletha's hand. She looked at me strangely. George made everyone bow their heads and close their eyes to show proper respect to his Holy Father. Guy didn't want to. An argument started. Finally, George mumbled quickly in one run-on sentence: "Godblessme-youronlySonourLordandthesemyfriendsandthegiftoffoodand-thehandsthatprepareditamen."

Gletha nudged Pud, who had fallen asleep during the prayer. The feast began. The conversation livened. Soon the troubled table guests began to laugh. Arguments were forgotten.

Then came the moment that was the very reason for the day itself—my mother's forced-casual announcement: "Well, I suppose it's time I brought it in."

The green bowl was taken from the top of the warm-water reservoir at the side of the stove, enshrined in its silver-plated rack, and processed to the table. As the cover was removed, the room was flooded with the sacred incense of the warm, golden-topped pudding.

There was an awed silence, deeper and more sacramental than ever graced a church. As my mother reached for the serving spoon, the silence was broken by Gletha's deep-throated admonition: "Wait!"

Every eye shifted to her imperious face. "We can't commune with the pudding while there's a break in the family circle. Stella's chair is empty."

There was a long silence. She returned her gaze to me. "Where's Stella?"

I squirmed in my chair and then responded, "I-I-I dunno'. Last time I saw her she was headed out to the barn to play with the kittens. I had to go to the toilet and when I came back she was gone and it was time for lunch and I figured she could take care of herself."

There seemed to be unspoken assent around the table to my point of view. Gletha was adamant. "We all get left out as it is by the folk out there. No way are we gonna' break the circle by leavin' out one of our own. Rogee, go to the barn and fetch Stella. We'll all wait right here 'til she comes."

I tried to scrunch myself small, but her eyes drilled into the very center of my soul. I slithered off my chair as unobtrusively as possible. No one at the table moved a muscle—including my mother, who, under less strained circumstances, was never motionless when guests were present. I slipped through the kitchen screen door. This was one of the only times in my life when I didn't let it slam. The table reverie must not be violated.

I dawdled through the woods, my mind whirling. I knew I was better than Stella at almost everything and I really did deserve some time alone without her obnoxious presence and it was my house and the bread pudding was baked by my mother and I ought to have some say in the matter of who was invited. In the presence of the sacred pudding, the touching hands and George's Father, however, such distinctions seemed to be wiped out.

I arrived at the shadowed clearing. Stella was still tied to the sapling. She was not crying or struggling. The setting sun broke into the deepening darkness, illuminating her for a moment. There was a peculiar grace about her as she stood there in captivity. I saw that her eyes were smiling at me. It seemed to be a smile of forgiveness.

I removed the bandanna from her mouth. Her only comment was a soft, "I knew you'd leave the battle and come for me." She made a movement with her bound arms as if wanting to hug me. I decided to untie her feet first, hoping her ardor would cool. As I bent down, a fresh odor accosted my nostrils. The potatoes in the apron pocket had begun to ferment. They smelled like my Cousin Dillard's forbidden potato wine.

Having freed her feet, I cautiously undid her arms. She looked at me appraisingly for a moment. The impending hug did not come. She reached into her apron pocket and took out two pieces of potato. She handed me one and ate the other immediately. The vegetable had softened. The offending crunch did not ensue. She looked at me expectantly. I owed her one. I gingerly consumed the potent morsel, discovering in the process that guilt and forgiveness can even transform the taste buds. She took my hand. We dawdled back through the gold-tinged forest.

Arriving at the house, we slipped quietly through the screen door. Stella paused automatically and chipped a piece from the icebox block. As we entered the dining room, the table scene was a wax museum tableau. The only movement was a slow drip of saliva from the corner of Uncle Guy's mouth as he contemplated the centered delicacy.

We slipped into our places. Gletha broke the silence by declaring, "I think we'd better re-pray." Hands touched and heads bowed. Stella extended her fist, which clutched the ice chip. I folded my hand around it and hoped for a short prayer because cold water immediately began to ooze down my bare arm. Gletha moved into one of her strange chants:

> Lord of the light,
> Lord of the dark,
> Lord of the leaf and the whole tree,
> Healer of circles and hungering hearts,
> From our brokenness make us free. AMEN.

My mother served a bit of the pudding to each guest. Uncle Guy held back his usual comment, "I'll take whatever's left in the bowl, Mary." Tears streamed down Mamie's face as her shattered mind focused for a moment on perfection. Uncle Babe took his plate and commented gently, "I ought to rub it on my leg. It looks good enough to heal."

I felt something in my hand. It was not a piece of ice this time—but rather a second shared slice of soft potato. Stella looked at me tenderly with smiling eyes. I was amazed at the transforming effect of bread pudding and wine-potato on my general attitude toward Stella.

Gletha looked trance-like at the green dish in its silver shrine. "I swear, Mary, every time I eat your bread pudding shaped by hands of love, I feel Jesus right here in this very room."

George turned to her and said softly, "Of course I'm here, Gletha." I was about to make a caustic, snickering, eight-year-old remark when, reading my look, she stopped me with a glance.

There were smiles all around as the guests prepared to leave. I glanced back at the table in the twilight. A dying ray of the red-gold setting sun touched the empty pudding bowl, and the final morsel of the sacred bread on a spoon suspended in mid-air, half-way to the mouth of my dozing Uncle Pud.

The Death of Otto Wickhorst

Gletha said he probably had to die. But did he really have to die that way? If Jesus saves, why couldn't he have saved Old Otto? But Gletha said that Jesus didn't save that way. And, maybe Jesus really had saved through me.

It happened like this. One mid-winter Sunday night, as a light snow fell, I waded through the deep drifts north of our shack. I climbed over the barbed wire fence and struggled toward the lumber camp bunkhouse. If I were lucky, there'd still be apple pie left from supper. Usually nobody ate the last piece because they knew "the kid" would be coming.

The lumberjacks were my special friends. Though they were, on occasion, brutal to each other, they never mocked my halting speech or shamed me because of my skinny body. Sunday nights were times of give-and-take. Through me they felt in touch with families left far away as they clustered there doing the only work available for miles around.

As I hit the path from the outhouse to the rear door of their temporary residence, Todd Racker slipped up behind me, grabbed my arms and flipped me in the air, imprisoning me on his shoulders. He ducked low going through the back door of the bunkhouse so I wouldn't crack my skull. He shouted, "I finally caught him—the apple pie thief. He was sneaking up from the left flank."

There was general laughter among the men. Bob Sharpless came up from behind, tickled me into limpness, took me from Racker's shoulders, folded me up into a ball and flipped me into another pair of waiting hands. I knew flight's freedom. I also knew they loved me, and I had no fear of falling. On one flight over the trestle table I saw the pie pan with *two* pieces of leftover pie.

At eight o'clock the gaming came to a halt. If the batteries in the radio were charged, we'd all gather 'round to listen to Charles E. Fuller and his "Old Fashioned Revival Hour." The men referred to him in a most familiar fashion as "Charlee." Fiddler Jake would play along with the radio studio organ while the men joined the choir. The splendid discord of "The Old Rugged Cross" echoed over the snowbound distance.

It must have been the discord which drew him to us. The choir had swung into a surprisingly lively rendition of "Amazing Grace." Fiddler Jake was inserting some dance motifs which would have been downright sinful to the self-righteous folk in Spruce Crossing at the Lakeside Church of Jesus Risen.

The men were singing lustily—though many were tone deaf from long hours of the sawmill blade's shattering whine. Having finished one piece of pie while they were otherwise occupied, I was surreptitiously reaching for the second when a sound stopped their singing and my excess.

A high tenor voice was adding a marvelous obbligato to the beloved hymn. There was unbelievable purity threatening the ill-kempt tonality of the praising woodsmen. We turned to its source. There, framed in the doorway, flecked with fresh-fallen snow, stood a dwarf-like figure clad in a hooded sheepskin greatcoat. It was carrying an ax wrapped in a gunny sack laced with binder twine in one hand and a worn duffel bag in the other. No face could be seen in the dim light of the smoky kerosene lamp. The sound simply floated out from the depths of the hood.

"Amazing Grace" came to a whispering close on the studio organ. Charlee moved directly into his weekly pitch for all his listeners to put dollar bills in envelopes and send them to him so that he might realize "his great dream in Pasadena, California." On this night, hands that usually headed pocketward were motionless in surprise at the strange intruder.

Clete Roberts, the camp foreman, recovered his voice first: "Did'ja just stop by to entertain us, or did'ja have something else in mind?"

The figure flipped back his hood. His face was sharply angled. His eyes burned into you. In certain shadows, his skull looked like the one on a lye can warning of poison. In a voice surprisingly deep he uttered one word, "**work**."

The men, having been threatened into silence by the beauty of the stranger's performance, now matched, to his decided disadvantage, the stranger's size with their usual tasks in the forest. They burst into harsh laughter to calm their uncertainty.

Paulie Patterson unfolded his six-foot-six-inch frame, rose, stretched and said, "Aren't you jist a wee tad small to even think about doing what needs to be done around here?"

The stranger turned his gaze upon Paulie and uttered two more words: "**Try me**."

Paulie folded up again into his chair as if the cutting tones touched scars of parental reprimands buried deep inside him.

Clete said, "Well, I suppose you can stay the night at least. Come morning, I'll give you a try in the timber. There's a cot empty over behind the stove. I can't guarantee the luck that goes with it. Ted Kinter had his back broke yesterday by a mis-felled tree. Now then, if you decide to stay, we might better at least know your name."

"Otto—Otto Wickhorst. And if that boy doesn't eat a second piece, I might take a shine to that apple pie. It's been many a day since my stomach's had anything really solid in it."

"Stow yer stuff and come on over and join us. We're havin' church with Charlee Fuller."

"I don't care for church. Too many lies. The music is okay. They can't tell lies easy-like in music."

He disappeared behind the stove in the farthest corner of the bunkhouse. We heard the back door close as he made his way to the two-seater down the path.

The men exploded: "Clete, you're a fool. We have no idea who he is. He might kill us all in our beds tonight. He's so puny we'll all have to do extra work. Anybody can see he's lazy."

Clete shouted them down. "I'm in charge here, and I'll work whoever I want to work!"

The men turned back to Charlee Fuller's choir, playing and singing along on "Rescue the Perishing." Otto returned down the back path. He raised his voice in praise of the churchless God. As he entered the room, he stopped his singing and headed for the table where I was still staring at the second piece of pie. He looked at me for a long moment.

"Well, kid, it looks like it's either you or me."

I eyed his gaunt face and listened to the dying strains of "Rescue the Perishing." I slid the pie pan, with its final piece, across the table toward him. He grinned—one of only two times I ever saw him smile. He stepped to the stove and poured a huge mug of the ever-present black coffee.

"What's yer favorite part of the pie?" he asked.

"I'm very fond of Cook Tom's crust."

"Yer a man of exquisite judgment." (I didn't know what the word "exquisite" meant, but I liked the tone of his voice.) He continued, "Back in the days when I used to go to Mass before I got smart, I always thought the Body of Christ should be served as beautiful, flaky pie crust rather than those stupid little cardboard wafers. (Again, I wasn't sure what he meant, but the Jesus I'd heard about would certainly have liked this pie crust.)

Otto attacked the delicacy hungrily. He paused for a moment and then carefully removed the great, thumb-marked curl of crust which rode the pie pan edge. He reached it across the table to me. He shoved the mug of coffee within my reach in case I needed a couple of swigs to wash the gift down. Having finished the crust, I reached for the mug, feeling very grown-up as I swallowed a mouthful of the gut-burning liquid. Otto's eyes held mine for a long moment—laughter glinting in them—but his face kept its mask of hiddenness. I wondered if we had not shared Mass right there at the bunkhouse table.

"The Old Fashioned Revival Hour" came to an end with a rousing rendition of "Jesus Saves." The other men in the room joined in with great vigor—but Otto remained strangely silent. The radio was turned off to save the batteries for the following evening's episodes of *The Lone Ranger* and *Lux Radio Theatre*. I had to catch a school bus early the next morning so I said good-night to Otto and the rest of the crew and waded back home. The snowfall had stopped. A harsh moon cast my shadow crookedly before me. As the wolves called in the distance, I wished that I were still riding Todd Racker's shoulders.

Chores, school and Sunday visits with the relatives kept me busy, so I had no news from my friends at the camp for a couple of weeks. One Friday I arrived home from school to find the house full of the smell of fresh-baked apple pies. Tom, the cook, had come to buy eggs from my mother. I had told her about the new arrival, his beautiful voice, sharing the pie—and my fear that the men would somehow drive him away. She sat Tom down with a cup of coffee and a piece of pie and the words, "It's always good to eat somebody else's bakin'." Having lured him into sitting for a while, she immediately began to quiz him. "How's that new man, Otto, working?"

"Well, he's *workin'* fine. In fact, he's a whirlwind in the woods. Ain't never had nobody who could down a tree faster. When he takes his double-bitted ax to the branches, it moves so quick you kin hardly see it. And sing—he sings all the time, like some opery star or somethin'. It's purty—but it kinda' gets on the men's nerves after a while. Now there ain't nobody on the crew who kin sing as good or timber as good. And then there's the nights. He keeps the lamp lit to all hours, drinkin' mug after mug of coffee and readin' outta' this big leather-bound book."

My mother cut in with high indignation, "I don't know what's come over all you men. A man should be allowed to read his Bible whenever he wants to without any complaints from the likes of you."

"But Mary, iffen it was the Bible, it'd be okay. But it's somethin' called *The Complete Works of William Shakespeare*."

My mother replied, "Well, maybe you owhoots could learn somethin' from him. Sure wouldn't hurt you none."

"Well, Mary, we didn't exactly want to learn anything. We wuz all right as we wuz."

I interrupted, "Is he still sleepin' in Ted K-K-Kinter's bunk behind the stove—or has he g-got a spot of his own now?"

Tom looked down at the floor, shuffled his feet a bit and mumbled, "Not really and yeah."

My mother picked up on this immediately. "I smell a skunk

in the woodpile. What have you roughnecks gone and done now?"

"Well, it warn't my idee. But, what with his stayin' up 'til all hours and all that singin' and makin' us all feel like nothin' in the woods 'cause he won't even take any breaks, and Old Clete thinkin' he was the best thing what ever swung an ax, Paulie Patterson decided that we best teach him his place."

Mother exploded, "Paulie Patterson! I never did like that no-good loudmouth. What's he gone and done now?"

"Well, Clete took a couple of days off to spend in town with his wife and kids. When night came, Old Otto drank his coffee and read his book while the rest of us played poker. I kept wishin' he'd go to bed 'cause my luck was down and I lost twelve dollars to Curley Martin. He finally went to Ted Kinter's bunk behind the stove and went to sleep. Now when Old Otto sleeps, he *really* sleeps. Ain't no wakin' him 'til mornin'. Soon as it was known that he was out, Paulie and Curley sprung into action. They...."

Tom abruptly cut off his narrative and began to get red around the ears. He continued, "Aw, Mary, I can't tell this part to no lady."

"Tom, there ain't much in this world I don't already know about—in particular when it comes to dumb fool stuff men do to each other. I think I know exactly what you did, but I want to hear it from your own shameful lips."

Tom stumbled on, getting redder as he went. "Well, Paulie and Curley went to the reservoir on the cookstove and dipped out a wash basin of nice warm water. We all tiptoed over around Ted Kinter's bunk—and Old Otto was dead asleep in it. Curley held the basin and Paulie took one of Otto's hands careful-like and slowly dipped it into the warm water. And...and...." By this time Tom's face was bright scarlet.

"And he...he...he peed in Ted's bunk. With all that coffee, a big wet stain soon came through the top of the covers. We wuz all standin' around with our fists in our mouths laughin', fit to be tied and tryin' not to be heard so's not to wake him up.

"Next mornin' Paulie got up early and waked the rest of us. We gathered 'round Ted's bunk ag'in. Old Otto stirred a little, opened his eyes—and sat bolt upright.

"Paulie said in this mock-sorry voice, 'Gee, Otto, we didn't know there was a hole in the ceiling over Ted's bunk. Must've been a unusually heavy rain in the middle of the winter to've soaked Ted's bunk that way.'

"Otto looked down. Then it hit him what'd happened—plus the fact that all of us was about to die laughin'. Bob Sharpless, who prize-fit for a while, put up his dukes to protect us when Old Otto came chargin' off the bunk to destroy us. He didn't charge. He just sat there—those grey eyes drillin' into ours. We all sorta' backed away. He didn't say nothin'. I just walked across the bunkhouse and began fryin' flapjacks. The other guys sat down at the table—nobody sayin' much of anythin'. Bob Sharpless stepped back to stoke up the stove and said later that Otto'd changed his longjohns and was throwin' his stuff in his bag. He never did come to the table to eat.

"Later in the day he appeared in the woods and cut timber like a maniac, but he didn't say a word to nobody. He didn't even sing. Some of us agreed that we kinda' missed it.

"Clete come back from town and sensed that something had happened. I think it had to a'bin Fiddler Jake who told him. Clete just came uncorked—threatened to fire Paulie. He walked over to Old Otto. I don't know what he said to 'im, but later on in the day when Jim Tompkins arrived to haul out a load of pulpwood, Clete stopped him and climbed into the cab with Old Otto. Later I heard tell that they first went to the sawmill and got a load of slabs which they carried up into that new piece of timber we were goin' to hit next, up beyond the scarlet fever family's graves. Then they went into town and got everythin' Old Otto would need to live by himself.

"Neither Clete nor Old Otto showed up for the next three days. On the mornin' of the fourth day, Clete appeared for breakfast. If looks could kill, we'd all be dead. He stood at the head of the table. Everybody could tell that this was somethin' important. The rest of the flapjacks went untouched.

"He said, 'Otto Wickhorst is the best timberman I've ever seen. He's a good man—a gentle man compared to some of the no-goods within the sound of my voice. A joke is a joke, but you destroyed somethin' inside him with your nonsense—you destroyed a piece of his pride. I invited him to work with this crew. I did not give you permission to shame him.

" 'I've helped him build a slab-and-tarpaper shack beyond Fever Pond. I've set him up with a grubstake. He wants to work alone—and if anyone of you tries to bother him, you're done with here.'

"When Clete spoke in that tone of voice, we all knew he meant business."

My mother interjected, "It's a sorry mess. I hope yer all satisfied. You know, Tom, you coulda' stopped the whole thing if you'd had any spine about you."

"I know it, Mary—but I didn't and what's done is done. There is just one other thing. I've run myself a trapline up around Fever Pond. Yesterday I was checkin' my traps. I heard the sound of his ax—and "Amazin' Grace" and "Jesus Saves" were ringin' out through the trees. Maybe some day I'll be able to reach out to him."

Tom picked up the crate holding twelve dozen eggs and headed out toward the bunkhouse.

My mind began to churn a mile a minute. I'd been up Fever Pond way many a time. I sure didn't want Otto to be completely alone. After all, we'd shared pie crust and coffee, and I knew how bad it was to have people make fun of you. I also knew what it felt like to be really alone.

"Mom, I've finished all my chores. I think I'll just run across the field to Gletha's. She wasn't feelin' too good yesterday. Maybe she needs some help milkin' the goats."

"I don't know why you spend all yer time hangin' around there—but it don't seem to hurt you none. You just get yerself back here in an hour."

My dad had gone to town, so I stopped to sneak a bale of alfalfa off the back of the stack. It had started to snow again, and the deer were hard put to find food. I dragged the bale to the edge of the field. Then I waded as fast as I could through the gathering darkness.

I paused at the goatshed. I heard Gletha singing one of her strange songs, the kind she always said gentled the goats so they'd let down their milk better. The three-legged grey cat sat expectantly by her side. She would occasionally direct the warm stream of milk from the goat's teat to the cat's mouth.

"Hi, Gletha. Can I help you?"

"No, this is the last 'un. You kin help me carry the pails to the house, though."

"Gletha, I gotta' tell you somethin'. The guys in the bunkhouse hurt a new man really bad—hurt him inside, which is the worst kind a' hurt."

To the sound of the goatmilk shushing into the pail, I told her the whole story. There was silence as I concluded my narration. She finished stripping the last drops from the goat's udder. Then she turned and looked at me. Her deep eyes were marred by tears.

Her voice came from far away. "They shouldna' done that. They shouldna' done that to any man. Sometimes you ain't got no more'n pride."

She rose from the low stool and handed me the bucket of milk. We walked across the clearing to the shack. Uncle Pud snored loudly behind the burlap room divider. She strained the milk through a piece of soft grey cloth into a large stone crock. She turned, took a loaf of fresh-baked bread from the shelf, cut a slice for each of us and broke off a piece of the sweet, nut-flavored goat cheese that I favored.

"Gletha, I can't leave him up there all by hisself. I've got to make sure he's all right. He's a sharer. I think us sharers gotta' stick together."

Gletha thought for a moment. "Tomorrow's Saturday. You got no school. Why don't you think about hikin' up there. You can take him a syrup pail of goatmilk and a loaf of bread, and yer ma would probably share something from the cellar with him—or maybe even one of those pies I could smell bakin' clear over here this mornin'."

"Gletha, he's a lot like you. He can't stand no church. Yet he keeps singin' about Jesus savin'. How do you s'pose that happens?"

"It has somethin' to do with crosses and love. But I guess the bunkhouse men have pretty much blocked themselves off from what that really means. Maybe *you* gotta' go up and do a little savin'."

"You know I'll go up, but I can't see how I can do any savin'. I'm not Jesus."

"Don't be too sure o' that. The cross is empty."

She was staring at me—her eyes black wells of mystery. I knew there was no use of my asking any questions.

The next day the sun was shining. A January thaw threatened. I hurried across the field to Gletha's. She poured me a Karo Syrup pail of goatmilk and handed me a loaf of bread. I had sweet-talked my mother out of a pie. Dad had slipped into one of his darknesses and was rocking aimlessly by the potbellied stove in the living room, his head in his hands. It occurred to me to wonder if maybe Jesus couldn't do something for him too.

It took about an hour to hike through the woods to Fever Pond. Tracks of deer, raccoon, wolves and rabbits intersected in the snow. As I neared the place where I thought Otto's shack might be, the sound of a saw, the whistle of a falling tree and the tattoo of an ax drew me in the right direction. Woven through the working sounds was Otto's voice belting out a gospel hymn:

> Sing above the battle strife:
> Jesus saves! Jesus saves!
> By his death and endless life,
> Jesus saves! Jesus saves!
> Sing it softly through the gloom,
> When the heart for mercy craves.
> Sing in triumph o'er the tomb:
> Jesus saves! Jesus saves!

I was so drawn into the sound that I didn't watch where I was going. Just as I spotted him about forty feet ahead, I stepped on a fallen dead limb. It cracked like a shot in the winter air. The ax stopped and Otto spun around in a crouch, ax poised, as if anticipating an attack. He saw me and relaxed.

He called out, "Well, if it ain't the pie-crust kid! C'mon over here."

I waded over to him through the crotch-deep snow. He came toward me and folded me up in an unexpected bear hug. I was scarcely able to keep the bucket upright and the bread and pie uncrushed. He kept an arm around me, and we headed for the little shack almost hidden in the trees.

"The shack ain't much, but it's real tight and enough for me. I got me a barrel o' kerosene for the lamp. The old well left from the folks that died up here of scarlet fever could be put back into shape. When Jim Tompkins hauled all this stuff up here before the loggin' trail drifted completely shut, he brung me enough food to get by on. Clete Roberts trusted me enough that I'd cut plenty of pulpwood to cover costs— and I already got more'n I need."

We stepped inside the shack. It contained a single room with a bunk built into one end, a small potbellied stove, a shelf and a table built into the remaining wall. There was a single rough stool and the bare necessities for cooking. On the table was a kerosene lamp with its glass globe freshly polished. By its side was *The Complete Works of William Shakespeare.*

"I brung you somethin' special."

I put the pie, bread and goatmilk on the table. He beamed.

"Let's have a piece of that pie right now."

"You go ahead. There's plenty more for me where that came from."

"I'll just do that. 'Sides, I only have one plate and one mug."

I rolled up a log from the pile beside the stove, set it on end and sat down. He reached for the coffee pot and poured part of a mugful of the blackest brew I'd ever seen—and filled it the rest of the way full with goatmilk. Then he looked at me—and carefully broke off a thumb-marked roll of dough which rode the edge of the pie pan. He slid the mug toward me, saying, "We can share."

When we'd finished the feast, I said, "Otto, did we just celebrate a—what did you call it—a Mass—something to do with remembering the savin' works of Jesus?"

Otto laughed strangely. "I think maybe we did after all."

We talked for a long time, carefully not mentioning the events that had driven him to this place. He told me stories about the animals he'd seen, especially how the beavers were working on the creek which ran into Fever Pond.

The sun's rays told me I needed to start for home. With Dad in his darkness, there would be extra cows for me to milk and more chores to do. As I left Otto, he seemed reluctant to let me go. He wanted assurances that I'd return.

I said, "Otto, are you sure you'll be okay up here all by yerself?"

"Oh, sure. I'll cut away at the timber. By the time the road thaws open, old Jim Tompkins will have to work all summer to haul it away! Besides, my saw and my ax, Will Shakespeare and me—there's a quartet to sing a song in the pine woods."

The rays of the westering sun lighted him as he stood waving in the doorway.

Some weeks passed before I headed back to the shack on Fever Pond. Each Sunday night the lumberjacks would inquire as to whether or not I'd seen Old Otto. They each privately confessed to me that they were sorry that they'd done what they did. They each swore to "make it up to Old Otto—some day." Cook Tom had just been up to run his traplines and commented that there'd been no sound around the shack, but he "hadn't wanted to disturb anybody."

It was the Saturday after Valentine's Day. I tucked inside my coat a red heart with lace around it which I'd made in school. Gletha gave me another pail of goatmilk. I'd "borrowed" a final piece of apple pie and headed off toward my friend.

As I neared the pond, there was a crash of a single falling tree, but no accompanying ax sounds. The beaver must have felled a streamside birch. I strained my ears to hear the familiar singing. Only silence greeted me.

I called out, "Hey! Otto! Come and get it: goatmilk and apple pie. It's the pie-crust kid!"

There was no welcoming response. I approached the tiny shack. I heard a strange rhythmic sound coming from inside: like the grate of a button-and-string-buzzsaw whirring on sandpaper. I pushed the door open. The temperature inside the shack was near freezing. Otto was huddled on the bunk, his breath rasping in and out. He was wrapped in the sheepskin greatcoat. His face, like a mask of death, was outlined in the hood.

"Otto! What's the m-matter?"

No answer shaped from the pained breathing. His hand beckoned me weakly toward the bunk. I placed my ear close to his lips. My hand found his forehead. He was burning with fever.

"Cold...too weak...fire" was all he could gasp.

I quickly stepped outside, chopped some kindling and soaked it with a little kerosene. Soon a fire was blazing in the small stove. I poured goatmilk in a pan. As soon as it was warm, I took a spoon and got some of it between his lips. He swallowed with great difficulty. I spooned as much as he would take.

He was now able to whisper. "The warmth feels good. I think my lungs are shot. There's coffee in the pot from three days ago. It'll be okay. Heat it up with the goatmilk."

I stepped to the stove and added the potent draught to the hot milk.

Otto whispered, "Didn't I hear you yelling something about pie when you came up?"

"Yeah, I brought you the last piece in the house."

He continued. I could hardly hear him: "I don't think I can eat anything—but I'd like just a flake of the crust."

I pulled the piece of pie from my pocket, unwrapped the wax paper and flaked off a bit of the crust onto his plate. The coffee/milk was simmering by this time. I filled his mug and stepped to the bedside.

"Rog—first of all promise me that you'll go to the bunkhouse and tell the men I forgive 'em—and ask 'em to forgive me for turnin' my back on 'em. There's not time in this life to turn your back on nobody."

His body was torn by a terrible cough. When it subsided he said, "Please, give me a little piece of the crust and say some special words of Jesus as you do it: 'This is my body broken for you.' And give me a sip of coffee, sayin' Jesus' words: 'This is my blood, shed for you'—and you drink a little in turn. That will give me the only healin' I really need."

We shared the crust and the cup. He seemed to breathe easier.

"Otto, I'm g-going to go and g-git Gletha. We gather lots of herbs together. She must have somethin' that'll make you well."

"No. Don't git nobody. I need to have you do one thing more before you go. I need to hear a word from Will Shakespeare. Can you read out loud?"

"Well, my stammer gets in the way of anythin' soundin' very

pretty. But I'll sure try. Then I'll go git Gletha.''

I reached for the book and opened it. The print was tiny, and I didn't know a lot of the words. "Where'd you want me to read?''

His breathing was harsher again, but he managed to gasp out, "In the back...some poems with numbers by 'em...called sonnets...read me the one numbered one-hundred and twenty.''

I turned to the back, found the poem and began to read. I so much wanted to please Otto. I stammered very little— even if I hardly understood a word I read:

That you were once unkind befriends me now,
And for that sorrow, which I then did feel,
Needs must I under my transgression bow,
Unless my nerves were brass or hammered steel.
For if you were by my unkindness shaken
As I by yours, you've pass'd a hell of time;
And I, a tyrant, have no leisure taken
To weigh how once I suffer'd in your crime.
O, that our night of woe might have remember'd
My deepest sense, how hard true sorrow hits,
And soon to you, as you to me, then tender'd
The humble salve which wounded bosoms fits!
But that your trespass now becomes a fee;
Mine ransom yours, and yours must ransom me.

I closed the book. Tears were streaming down his face. I knelt by his bunk and wrapped my arms around him and held him close for a moment. I put some more wood on the fire and turned to go—when I remembered. I reached inside my coat and pulled out the slightly crumpled red heart with the lace around it. I slipped the edge between two slabs at the foot of his bed.

"Thanks. That'll remind me of the sacred heart of Jesus and of you.''

I turned and rushed out into the sunlight. I waded as fast as I could through the snow toward Gletha's. I rushed into her shack.

"Gletha! Otto Wickhorst's d-d-dyin'. You've g-got to put some herbs together that'll loosen his chest and make his fever come down. Hurry! We may be too late already!"

"Quiet down, boy. There's lots worse things than death."
She moved to the shelves where the fruits of our gathering
labors were stored. She selected three or four and wrapped
them quickly into a pouch at her waist. She wrapped two more
layers of the cloths around her. She passed one end around
me, circled me with her arm, and we moved off toward Fever
Pond. We seemed to scarcely touch the snow.

It felt like only moments before we were standing at the
door of Otto's shack. We stepped in. The cabin was warm. No
sound came from the bunk. Otto lay motionless. The labored
breathing had stopped. His face was a mask of death framed
in the hood of the sheepskin greatcoat. He was smiling.

I started to cry. Gletha held me for a moment and then said,
"I see there's a piece of pie here that you musta' just brought.
Nothin' we can do for Otto. Might as well git some strength
for the journey home."

"Good!" I replied. "We can finish the pie, the crust in particular, and have some coffee/milk—and finish the Mass."

Gletha looked at me quizzically but said nothing. Having
finished our refreshments, we wrapped ourselves in the soft
grey cloths and floated through the darkening forest.

Later that evening, I walked over to the bunkhouse to tell
the men of Otto's death. The poker playing and coarse
laughter came to a halt. After a moment's silence, each of
them shared what he wished he'd done. I left them with their
thoughts and walked home in the moonlight.

The following day, being Sunday, the loggers decided to go
up to Fever Pond and see what they could do. Cook Tom
stopped at our shack and invited me along. I threw on my
sheepskin coat and followed the silent processional. Fiddler
Jake carried his fiddle in its case. Some men carried picks
and others shovels. Clete Roberts remembered a caved-in
root cellar near the well. It might prove to be a burial place
in spite of the frozen ground.

Clete's memory was right. The men took turns with the
picks and shovels and soon a place was ready. Then, Paulie
Patterson and Bob Sharpless lifted Otto tenderly from the
bunk. They placed him on a couple of leftover slabs, and we
all proceeded to the grave site. Fiddler Jake had his instru-

ment ready. Otto was placed lovingly in the grave which Todd Racker had lined with fresh pine boughs.

Fiddler Jake began "Jesus Saves." The men sang the words softly as they sobbed. Some of them could hardly make it through the line, "When the heart for mercy craves."

I stepped to the edge of the grave and said, "Otto asked me to read this to him just before he died."

I opened Will Shakespeare to sonnet one-twenty and read, "That you were once unkind befriends me now...." When I finished, Tom, the cook, said quietly, "I didn't understand all o' that, but I think it has somethin' to do with what we done to him."

"Well," I said, "he asked me to tell you that he forgave you, and he wanted you to forgive him for leavin' you. There's just not enough time in life for folks to turn their backs on one another."

Fiddler Jake played hymns while the men filled in the grave. Then Todd Racker threw me up on his shoulders, and we headed in silence back to the bunkhouse.

Nobody but me noticed Gletha, the goatlady, step from the shadow of the woods, enter the shack and come out with the lace-edged valentine in her hands. She walked to the grave and put the heart in the center of the mound, weighting it with a small stone. Then she disappeared into the trees.

Hosea and Christmas

It was Mayetta Mahan Tolliver who started the tradition. Let me tell you about Mayetta Mahan. She was *not* from Bear Run Township. She came from three townships down, and it was rumored that her folks had money. It was also rumored that they lived in a two-story house. Someone whispered one day that they even had indoor toilets, a phenomenon not experienced in our neighborhood.

Mayetta often came up to Bear Run to visit her cousin, Flossie Billups. It was on one of those visits that she met Todd Tolliver.

There was no church for miles around. However, Flossie had taken a Voice of Prophecy Home Bible Study Course: The Entire Bible in Fifty-two Easy Lessons. It was generally assumed that Flossie knew everything there was to know about the Good Book. She never did anything to allow that assumption to be questioned.

A group of folks gathered in Flossie's living room every Friday evening to partake of her accumulated knowledge. When visiting, Mayetta always provided refreshments for the group. No one was quite sure which was most welcome: her presence or the pan of her legendary blueberry buckle. It always seemed that the lesson was cut a bit short when Mayetta was there. The incense emanating from the delicacy in the center of the table depressed the appetite for the Word and sharpened the appetite of the flesh.

One Friday evening in late October the group was increased

by four unexpected students: Mayetta Mahan; Gletha, the goatlady, with me in tow; and Todd Tolliver. I'd heard my older cousins snickering about the fact that Flossie's Bible study class was going to discuss the book of Hosea which was "all about whores and stuff and what was old Flossie going to do with that?" I knew that Gletha read the Bible a lot by herself. She didn't want it ruined by churches and preachers and hypocritical folk who were always casting her out by suggesting that she was a witch. I went to her to check out my cousins' comments. Gletha's face became sad when I indicated their tone of voice.

"It's the most beautiful book in the whole Bible," she said, her voice touched with quiet wonderment. "It's about folk being forgiven and about the mercy of God. I think maybe you and me oughta' slip into the class tonight just to make sure Flossie understands what it's really about."

"Gletha, they won't want us there," I protested. "Are you sure they'll even let us in the door?"

She looked at me deeply for a moment. "If they don't, we'll know that they don't understand the meaning of the book."

Arriving early so that our presence might not be so starkly noted, we walked up to the Billup's sprawling house. It had been added onto many times to accommodate eleven children. Now that they were all "growed and gone," some of the inside partitions had been removed to make the largest gathering place in the township next to Bear Run School. As Flossie opened the door and stared at us in surprise, another student commented a bit too loudly, "I wonder what the old witchlady and that snot-nosed kid are doing here."

Gletha provided the answer. "We come to work through the Word of the Lord with all of you."

Flossie was caught. She ushered us in and took us to a far corner of the room where a worn easy chair and a three-legged stool were unoccupied. In a quick motion she removed a freshly starched crocheted piece from the chair back which pictured a leaping deer and the carefully worded Gothic lettered motto: "Welcome to Our Happy Home." (She later explained to my cousin, Margaret, that she "didn't want her new-done piece ending up smelling of goats.")

The predominant smell in the room was not of the goats

but of indescribable incense. It was a subtle combination of cinnamon, nutmeg and cardamom. I turned my head so that my eyes could follow the unerring direction of my nose. I saw it. There at the far end of the room on the refreshment table illumined by Flossie Billup's best kerosene lamp with the milk-glass shade was the reason for the excitement of my taste buds. In the biggest baking pan I'd ever seen was an incredibly high-risen cake with rich crumb topping swirled with blue syrup. It had to be Mayetta Mahan's legendary blueberry buckle.

The fact was confirmed when a young woman I'd not seen before came in from the kitchen carrying a bowl of whipped cream. Next to Pauline Pucharski, she had to be the prettiest woman I'd ever laid eyes on. She was dressed in a dark orange frock that certainly was not made of printed feed sacks from the elevator. Her hair was a deep, deep brown. It was parted in the middle and fell forward on her shoulders in two thick, perfect curls. As folk arrived, her smile melted anyone who might, under other circumstances, have made a whispered comment about the newcomer "puttin' on airs." Many of the women brought a little something for the refreshment table, including molasses cookies, brown bread with wild strawberry jam, an angel food cake swirled with seven-minute icing. Everything paled in significance to that which was enthroned in the center of the table.

Among the last to arrive was Todd Tolliver. He'd come down from the Pine Mountain Lumbering Camp to spend a couple of days with his dad. Paul Tolliver lived alone in a tiny cabin about a hundred yards from the Billups'. Todd's mother had died when he was seven. A couple years back a mis-felled tree had shattered his dad's right leg. It healed so badly that he could no longer work the timber. He had a bit of old-age pension, and Todd shared his meager earnings. Flossie kept an eye on him. He spent most of his days carving Paul Bunyan figures (he always said he'd been named for "Big Paul"). They were sold in Bear Run Store to hunters and fishermen who came up from the Twin Cities.

Todd came in the back door of the house. He saw me and Gletha first in our obscure corner almost beyond the light from the four kerosene bracket lamps mounted in front of their metal reflectors on the walls around the room. He walked over, pulled Gletha from her chair and enfolded her in a great bear hug. Word was that when his ma died years before, he'd roamed the woods with Gletha just like I did now. Then Gletha and Pud had moved away. After that, with his dad away in the timber so much, Todd always said he'd raised himself. He was well over six-feet tall, with a thick, soft black beard that matched his curly hair and deep-set eyes. In his mid-twenties, intensely quiet, with a voice that reflected the thunder's rumble when he did on occasion speak, Todd Tolliver was the object of hope for every young unmarried woman in Bear Run Township.

Releasing Gletha, he pulled up a second three-legged stool and hunkered down on the other side of her. She took one of our hands in each of hers and muttered something about "her boys." Todd looked over at me and winked, making me feel good all over. I needed a big brother right bad. I wished he wasn't gone 'most all of the time in the timber.

Then Todd began to sniff. "Unless somebody sprinkled cinnamon in my beard while I napped a while ago, I'd say there was something far beyond the usual on Flossie's table tonight."

He looked up and saw the legendary blueberry buckle and Mayetta Mahan at the same time. Gletha flinched as Todd gripped her hand. Mayetta locked eyes with him for a long moment, then turned and floated to the kitchen, returning in a moment with a pot of coffee.

Mayetta sat down at the head of the table as Flossie got everybody's attention: "Well now, folks, we're going to do things a little different tonight. We're going to eat first and do the Word second. I'm real glad to welcome my cousin back with us. Most of you know Mayetta Mahan. She's just made my kitchen glow this afternoon helpin' me get ready for all of you. Such an extra good crowd tonight. Got no idea why. We're just going to do a little studying of the Word together. Oh, yes. Todd—it's real good to have you down from camp. Your daddy's always terrible glad to see you. Now, everybody just come up to the table before the blueberry buckle gets cold and the whipped cream falls. Make sure you have some cake and bread and cookies as well. I have a feeling everything's extra good tonight."

There was a general movement toward the table. Todd, Gletha and I held back. We listened to the exclamations concerning the table's centerpiece. When we finally arrived at our destination, there were only two servings left of the legendary blueberry buckle. Gletha smiled at Mayetta and said she'd be satisfied with just the wonderful smell of the delicacy and helped herself to a piece of angel food cake. I took a plate and was about to receive a piece of the blueberry buckle when a look from Gletha stopped me. I settled for a couple of molasses cookies and faded back to watch what was going to happen next.

Mayetta turned to Todd and said, "I don't believe we've ever met. I'm Mayetta Mahan."

Todd responded with a quiet rumble, "I'm Todd Tolliver."

Again, they simply looked at each other for a long moment. Gletha was also watching. Mayetta took her server and gracefully lifted the remaining portions to Todd's waiting plate and topped them with a mountain of whipped cream. He grinned his thanks, followed by, "Thank you, ma'am." You could tell from Mayetta's face that she felt she'd just been thanked by the prince of the pulpwood cutters.

Gletha commented quietly, "I think we just had a troth plighted without a parson." I didn't know what those words meant, but I didn't need to. Something special had certainly happened. Watching Todd's face as he returned to his stool was like watching a man lighted up by a candle in the dark, except that in his case the fire was inside.

Just before he folded himself onto the stool, he looked down at me for a long moment. I just sat there grinning foolishly up at him. He slid one portion of the blueberry buckle onto my plate and said with teasing ferocity, "That's hush-buckle, kid. I don't want you speculating about nothing to nobody."

It was not the most ideal event for two people to fall in love at, what with the general topic for the evening being how in the world God could ask a man to marry a prostitute and then her leaving him after bearing his children and finally him buying her back. Mayetta remained seated at the head of the table. When the conversation got particularly racy, I noticed they were both blushing. Flossie had a bit of trouble getting the discussion beyond the first three chapters of the book to where Hosea talks about nations who go a'whoring and how God feels. Folk seemed to want to dwell on the juicier parts of the narrative.

Finally, Flossie decided to terminate the discussion by posing a general question: "You were all supposed to have come prepared by having read the Book of Hosea which is only fourteen chapters. I'd like some comments, one at a time, about what the last eleven are all about."

There was dead silence. Flossie looked helplessly around the room and then at her Bible notes from the Voice of Prophecy which were, at the moment, not standing her in very good stead. Then Gletha stood up. The uncertain light of the kerosene lamps dimly illuminated the flowing grey cloths with which she wrapped herself. She looked for all the world like one of those goddesses carved from marble pictured in our mythology book at school. The gathering sensed her movement. Every neck craned to get a better look at what the witch woman was going to do and say next. Gletha began: "Flossie, it's really all about forgiveness—us forgivin' each other and God forgivin' us—no matter what. Remember, it says in 11:9: 'I will not execute the fierceness of mine anger. I will not return to destroy Ephraim; for I am God and not man, the Holy One in the midst of thee; I will not come to destroy.' And in 6:1 Hosea says, 'Come, let us return unto the Lord, for he hath torn, and he will heal us; he hath smitten, and he will bind us up.' This little book is probably the most important book in the whole Bible because it happens we're to forgive like God does in 14:4: 'I will heal their backsliding, I will love them freely; for mine anger is turned away from them.' "

Gletha turned, tugged at my sleeve, and we left the gathering by the rear door of the house. The late autumn frost glistened in the light of the full moon. As we walked the wordless distance to Pud and Gletha's shack, the feet of scurrying small animals whispered in the forest. An owl's shadow flashed across the scene.

As we stepped through the door, the abrasive waves of

Pud's snoring seemed to make the burlap curtain which separated their double bed from the rest of the one-room shack move back and forth. As I listened to the familiar sound, I almost decided that there's a thing or two in this life that's eternal after all.

I polished off a cup of goatmilk warmed on the wood-burning stove. I told Gletha I was real proud of her fine speech at the end of the evening. She only said, "I'm not sure any of those folk—or us for that matter—understand what the Word in the flesh is really all about."

As I headed home across the moonlit field, I saw two figures walking in the distance. I stepped into the shadow of the pines until they passed by. It was Todd Tolliver and Mayetta Mahan. They were so intent on each other that they didn't see me. I turned to hurry back to Gletha's and tell her what I saw. The taste of the "hush-buckle" rose up in my memory. I continued steadfastly toward home. I never speculated about nothing to nobody.

Mayetta Mahan became a semi-permanent guest at Flossie's. Todd Tolliver needed to be with his father two or three times a week. There's not much way to hide the flow of events in Bear Run Township. It was announced after a whirlwind courtship that Mayetta and Todd would be married on the 15th of December.

It was then that Mayetta Mahan Tolliver began the tradition. She suggested to folk that wouldn't it be nice to gather in Bear Run School on Christmas Eve and have a celebration. We could all bring a little something to share. Everybody knew the table would be crowned by her legendary blueberry buckle. Fiddler Jake could play, and we could all do a little dancing to show our joy at the holy birth. Then we'd all get real quiet, and the family with the baby born nearest Christmas would dress in special costumes which she'd sew with her own hands. They'd take their places in the center of the schoolroom. We'd all stand 'round, and someone would read the Christmas story from Luke. Then we'd sing Christmas carols, and someone would send us all home with a prayer.

Scarcely was the wedding over when Mayetta began to sew furiously for the Christmas celebration. A midnight blue robe for Mary was created out of real silk sent to her by an uncle who had been a missionary in China. A robe of grey homespun would grace the shoulders of stalwart Joseph. She didn't need to sew anything for Baby Jesus. Her mother gave her a long baptismal robe worn by her great-grandfather before the Civil War.

As Mayetta sewed, she dreamed. This first Christmas would see Mark, Anne and baby Tom Steele as the center of attention. However, if there was one thing she'd wanted more than Todd, it was to bear and nurture Todd's baby. To be the Holy Family next year—or surely the year after—would be the climax of their dream together.

The celebration was indeed wondrous. The food was as beautiful as the economy would allow. Some of it rivaled—but never surpassed—the legendary blueberry buckle which filled the room with its sacred incense of cinnamon, nutmeg and cardamom. My Aunt Jennie, vital as a girl at eighty-five, read the Christmas story like it had never been read before. We really saw the Baby (little Tom remained blissfully silent), the Holy Mother (Anne's blonde hair shown in the lantern light like a halo in contrast to the midnight blue of her robe) and the foster-father, Joseph (Mark shuffled his feet a bit in nervous embarrassment, wishing he was back in the woods cutting timber—but we all guessed Joseph, the carpenter, probably had done the same thing when the kings arrived and kneeled). When the reading was done, Fiddler Jake began "Silent Night" softly on the fiddle while everybody sang. Only Gletha and I were really aware of Mayetta and Todd, off in a shadowed corner of the room. They were holding each other gently. Mayetta had a beatific smile on her face. Todd couldn't take his eyes off the sleeping infant in the center of the room. As everyone bundled up to return to their homes, singing "We Wish You a Merry Christmas," some of the folk teased the newlyweds as they left with: "Maybe next year you'll all be in the center." Todd and Mayetta only smiled and dreamed together. Everyone in Bear Run Township knew as they left that a Christmas tradition had been born that night which would be with them in joy for years to come.

The crisis happened a week after Christmas. Todd returned to the lumber camp up Pine Mountain, promising Mayetta he'd be back within the week. A heavy storm blocked the men for six days. The second day of the blizzard Todd awakened with a fever. He was encouraged to remain in his bunk, and it didn't take a lot of encouragement. As the day wore on, the fever increased and the glands beneath his jaws began to swell. There was good-natured kidding about poor Toddy and his mumps. Everybody did everything they knew how to bring the fever down, but nothing seemed to work. The days wore on. Todd had moments of delirium. The men massaged him with snow. There was only momentary relief. Finally, on the fourth day the swelling began to diminish a bit in his neck. However, he began to feel pain in his testicles. Soon his scrotum stretched taut. He asked someone to fetch Gletha. She'd have a cure of some sort. But the blizzard continued with full force.

The malady ran its course along with the storm. When the weather cleared, the loggers rigged a traverse, wrapped the exhausted, emaciated Todd in blankets, donned their snowshoes and pulled him down to the cluster of cabins around the store and the school.

Mayetta and Gletha nursed him back to full health and strength. About a month later Gletha had some "woman talk" with Mayetta. Gletha broke the high probability to her firmly but gently. The mumps, having "gone down" on Todd, had killed most of his living seed. Though he would continue to love her in all the ways a man should, he might never be able to father a child.

Mayetta wept while Gletha held her. Heading back to their cabin, she found Todd splitting wood. Sensing that she'd been crying, he reached out and folded her into his arms. The harsh screams of the blue jays in the pine branches above them formed a counterpoint to the harsh issue they discussed in the snow-covered clearing. Todd kept assuring Mayetta that he would be all right. They would, indeed, have a child. They would have the place of honor in the newly begun Christmas tradition in Bear Run School. They assured each other that they were enough in love that childlessness would never really make any difference. Yet something in their eyes was shadowed.

When Christmas Eve arrived the following year, everyone

gathered in Bear Run School. Their noses were greeted with the familiar welcome of cardamom, cinnamon and nutmeg. There on the table center was the legendary blueberry buckle surrounded by the somewhat lesser offerings. The eating and dancing progressed well. Linda and Darrell Smith and little Alma then took their places in the middle of the room. Aunt Jennie read and the carols were sung. Mayetta smiled a lot in a sort of forced way. Todd remained in the shadows. At one point in the evening, Gletha paused by him and said, "I'm going to give you a Christmas hug like when you was a little boy." She proceeded to wrap an end of soft grey cloth around him. He wept soundlessly.

The following Christmas, the tradition and its familiar smells, dances, carols and readings flowed out, lifting the hearts of everyone. When Peter and Millie Carlson donned the grey and blue robes and wrapped their five-month-old son, Chipper, in the elegant antique Baptismal garb, the folk all thought it was the prettiest Nativity they'd ever seen. When Chipper sat up laughing and crowing during Aunt Jennie's Bible reading, everyone agreed that "they'll have to watch that one. He's going to be a real live wire."

Mayetta was at the party. She seemed thin and distant. Word had it that Todd was accepting jobs at logging camps further and further away. His times with Mayetta were fewer and farther between. I asked her where he was tonight, and she said, "He had a terrible throat and just didn't feel like comin'."

It was finally agreed that Todd would remain home during the month of January and pick up some odd timbering jobs closer to Bear Run.

It was the second week of the month when the flyers arrived in our mailboxes. The Lakeside Church of Jesus Risen in Spruce Crossing was going to have a full week of evangelistic services. We would all be privileged to hear the Reverend Billy Bundy who had spent most of his life bringing souls to Christ "from the jungles of darkest Africa to the igloos of Alaska." Reverend Bundy's picture showed an intense-eyed man with slicked-back dark hair, sober-facedly praising the God of joy.

Since there was little to do in Bear Run Township during

the deepest days of winter and the roads had been plowed, it was agreed that most of the folk wanted to be there. We loaded our cars tightly and proceeded toward our destination intent on breaking the monotony and recharging our spiritual batteries. I tried to get Gletha to go. She said that somebody had to stay at home and hold the world together. She drifted off into the gathering darkness.

As we entered the parking lot, we were impressed by the huge black Cadillac with New York plates parked right up next to the church. A passing worshiper assured us that it belonged to the visiting evangelist himself. As we entered the church, we were coldly welcomed by the townsfolk. Todd, Mayetta and I sat together in one of the back pews. We worried a bit about whether or not we could hear. Our fears on that score were allayed by the entrance of Billy Bundy. As the piano crescendoed, Billy stepped out onto the chancel and began to sing. His voice seemed to challenge both the gates of heaven and hell. When he said, "Let us pray," we were treated to a short course of theology and witness. When he began to preach and said the word "Jesus," he did it in such a way that the hair on the back of my neck began to caterpillar. When he made a passing comment about hell, I lost every ounce of desire to ever want to visit firsthand.

At the end of the sermon, he issued a call to his listeners to come forward and give their hearts to Jesus. I remained rooted to my pew, afraid to move and afraid not to. Todd's face showed unabashed disapproval. Mayetta was not to be discouraged. She moved forward and took her place with assurance. She knelt down at the railing. It was a good scene to watch from a distance. Billy Bundy spent a few moments in prayer with each one who gave his or her heart to Jesus. It seemed to me that he gave a bit more time to the ladies as he knelt with them. When he came to Mayetta, he spent a lot more time wrestling with Satan for her immortal soul.

As Mayetta came back to her seat, her face glowed with a kind of inner peace we all need to feel once in a while. She said, "I'm comin' back tomorrow night. So many things I've got to get right with God."

The following evening, Mayetta hooked a ride with the Carlsons. Todd and I stayed behind and played checkers.

Todd confided in me that he saw Billy Bundy as a fraud, and there was no way he'd ever even walk across the street to hear him again.

When Mayetta returned from the second evening of inspiration, she was radiant as she sat down to regale us with all the details of the wondrous skills of Billy Bundy. She now had hope of someday the entire world coming to Jesus.

Mayetta didn't miss a meeting the entire week. Todd remained stolidly behind. On the final night, Saturday, Mayetta didn't come home. The Carlsons were sure she had caught a ride with the Smiths, and the Smiths were equally sure that she'd caught a ride with the Carlsons. When he called everybody he could think of who had been at the meeting, Todd jumped in his battered truck and, taking me and Gletha with him "for company," raced to Spruce Crossing. The black Cadillac with the New York plates was gone. The Lakeside Church of Jesus Risen was dark. The only sound was the discordant cries of the blue jays disturbed by the midnight interlopers.

Four days later he received a two-line message from Mayetta: "I loved you deeply. Now I love another and the Jesus I sense inside him."

Todd was devastated. He couldn't bring himself to face folk. He wouldn't play checkers with me. Gletha would drop by their shack on occasion just to hold him in her arms like she had when he was a little boy.

Todd left the logging camp, deserted their cabin and went to cut timber alone, living in the shack where Otto Wickhorst had died. Rumors flowed back to Bear Run Township through Flossie from Mayetta's mother. Billy and Mayetta were in Florida. Then they were in Oklahoma. Shortly after they left, it was rumored that she was pregnant. Then word came that he had deserted her in Texas, leaving her penniless. He used all their resources to get to the Congo to preach Jesus crucified and risen to the heathen in the far-flung lands. Mayetta, it was rumored, had hitched rides until she got back to her folks.

Gletha made sure that Todd was aware of all of this. On good days we'd hike through the forest to Fever Pond and take him some goatmilk and cheese and some fresh-baked bread. He assured us that his love for Mayetta was over and that he never wanted to see her again because he could never, in his wildest dreams, forgive her. He wanted to continue to build his life alone without her.

As Christmas approached, nobody in Bear Run Township wanted to give up the tradition. It had been a strange year. No new babies had been born. Flossie had the costumes at her house, and she agreed to co-ordinate the affair. The Carlsons decided that they could do the Holy Family again if they could just catch Chipper at the right moment to be the Baby Jesus.

Gletha and I went up to see Todd the week before Christmas. Gletha told him that if he was serious about building a new life he had better come back to civilization once in a while. There were still unattached young women who were waiting for him to stop his grieving. He said he'd never marry again, crippled as he was. Gletha did convince him to come down for Christmas Eve and for him and his dad to eat with her and Pud on Christmas Day.

When Christmas Eve arrived, all of Bear Run Township converged on Bear Run School. There'd been a bit more work in the woods so everyone had been generous with what they brought by way of food to share. When people arrived, they were greeted by the usual incense of cinnamon, cloves and cardamom. There was general relief that Mayetta had given somebody the recipe before she left. It just wouldn't be Christmas without blueberry buckle.

Todd Tolliver sat far back in the corner, out of reach of the kerosene lantern lights which illumined the room from several sources. His dad sat with him part of the evening and part of the evening called the square dances as Fiddler Jake fiddled them.

When it became time for the Nativity scene, Peter and Millie Carlson donned the special robes of grey and midnight blue. With considerable effort, Chipper was caught to be the Baby Jesus. No one attempted to wrap him in the antique robe. The prophecy from the year before had been right. He had indeed become "a real live wire."

All the lanterns were extinguished except the one hanging over the Nativity itself. As Aunt Jennie rose to once again do the Christmas story from Luke, a sound was heard and the revelers felt a rush of cold air. Turning toward the schoolhouse door, they saw her silhouetted against the light from the full moon: Mayetta Mahan Tolliver with her baby in her arms.

There was total silence. Even Chipper stopped struggling in his daddy's arms. Todd rose from his chair and tried to move toward the back door of the school. He was stopped by Gletha who took him in her arms just like she had when he was a little boy. She whispered two words which only I heard, standing as I was by her side: "Remember Hosea."

Mayetta walked slowly toward the circle of light in the center of the room. The Carlsons moved off the stool and melded into the crowd of onlookers. Mayetta sat down wordlessly, her head bowed over her infant son. Millie Carlson stepped forward and draped the midnight blue robe around Mayetta's shoulders. The crowd parted like the Red Sea as Todd began to slowly move toward her. As he passed Peter Carlson, Peter handed him the Joseph robe of grey homespun. Todd stepped into the lantern light, the robe around his shoulders. Everyone could see tears streaming down his face. Mayetta turned and held the baby out to him. She said softly, "I named him Hosea."

Todd Tolliver cradled the baby in one arm and placed his other arm around Mayetta, holding her close as Aunt Jennie began to intone the Christmas story from Luke. At its close, Fiddler Jake softly played "Silent Night."

When the carol drew to an end, the music was completed by the voice of Gletha, the goatlady, who had stepped behind Todd, Mayetta and the baby: "There's another passage of Scripture that needs to be remembered this Christmas Eve. It's Hosea 6:1: 'Come, let us return unto the Lord, for he hath torn, and he will heal us; he hath smitten, and he will bind us up.' "

Todd, Mayetta and baby Hosea moved out of the light, through the lingering incense of cinnamon, cloves and cardamom, through the schoolhouse door and into the midnight light of the full moon.

Something Like Resurrection

Bear Run Store was a place of wonder. It stood at the crossroads above Bear Run School. A penny would produce a miraculous draught of horehound drops and licorice sticks. A dill pickle fresh from the barrel and nestled between saltine crackers kept hunger pangs from overcoming many a school child.

The wide, open porch with its decaying railing was always occupied, from the first spring anemone poking through the snow to the last leaf in fall, by a varied assortment of neighborhood men. My Uncle Guy could often be seen, a heavy wad of Copenhagen snuff proving no barrier to tales of mermaids observed while sailing to France to fight in the war to end all wars. Pulpwood cutters and failing farmers and fur trappers were driven inside by zero temperatures to continue the shaping and swapping of myths which grew more wonderful with each retelling. The old hunters paralyzed children with tales of attacking timber wolves who would strike the lonely forest-wanderers, leaving only the buckles of their bib overalls extant on the forest path.

Presiding over the changing scene was Aunt Minnie T. She'd kept order in the establishment for thirty-one years—ever since her husband Ned had been killed in a sawmill accident. The gory details of his death were a favorite evening's recitation. Aunt Minnie always listened proudly, knowing that nothing had ever happened in the whole county which could match the sheer terror of Ned's demise.

Aunt Minnie T. lived by a stern behavioral code: no drinking, no fighting and no spitting on either the floor or the cast iron stove which glowed red from dawn to dusk when the cold grasped the countryside. Sometimes a lumberjack would try to sneak a drink from a pocket-flask—only to feel a slap " 'side the head" from her calloused hand and receive the dreaded expulsion from the social oasis in the wilderness. She did all of this from the vantage point of a stature which never quite touched five feet nor tipped the scales at a hundred pounds.

Gletha, the goatlady, would often appear in the shadows of the porch or in a dark corner of the store. She would bring Karo Syrup pails of goatmilk to be sold over the counter. Intent on the flow of words, the gathered community would not notice her arrival. The speaker of the moment, however, would sense her intense brown eyes upon him. Soon, he would find himself winding down into an embarrassed silence. In the ensuing quiet, she would disappear as quickly as she came—pausing only to press a coin into Aunt Minnie's ever-ready hand for a pound of sugar or a box of lard. The store would quickly empty since no more words were forthcoming.

Mel Zilitz, who worked for Aunt Minnie and slept in a dirty little room in the back of the store, summed up the situation nicely: "I sure wish that crazy witchwoman would leave us alone. She just stands there staring the truth into us!"

"Now, Mel," Aunt Minnie responded, "she's harmless—and her money is a lot better'n your credit. 'Sides, all you freeloadin' windbags are about to empty my pickle barrel and peanut sacks without my havin' anything to show for it."

The winter of '42 will never be matched in the minds of those who braved the huge drifts and bitter temperatures. The sun shone with particular brightness that February day when, leaving Mel behind the counter, Aunt Minnie T. climbed into her '36 Ford. She headed for Spruce Crossing, thirty miles away, to load up with snuff and staples while the road was still briefly clear of the deep snow. She had not been gone a half hour when, as if Mother Nature had flicked a heavenly switch, the sun went out behind heavy storm clouds. The air filled with wildly swirling flakes. The road in front of the store disappeared.

After eighteen hours, the snow stopped. The usual inhabitants of Bear Run Township waded to their favorite place of refuge from winter boredom. Everybody knew that Aunt Minnie had found a welcome bed in town and would return in triumph behind the first county snowplow.

About ten o'clock the following day, a roar was heard in the distance. Pickles, peanuts and tales were quickly forgotten as the clutter of men fastened up their sheepskin coats and headed for the porch to give the brave Aunt Minnie T. a heroine's welcome for risking the winter road so that their snuff-expectant cheeks need not go unoccupied.

The huge piece of machinery came into view, tearing down and re-shaping white mountains on the roadsides. The men cheered and strained their eyes into the distance to discover the approaching Aunt Minnie T.

Suddenly, as if by some strange act of levitation, Gletha, the goatlady, appeared. The light wind drifted an eddy around her as if the Queen of the Snow had carried her there in her private carriage. Gletha watched Tom Geddy climb from the cab, his face a sad mask. She disappeared around the machine in the opposite direction.

"Some of you men, come quick," he called. "It's Aunt Minnie T. Her car slid off the road into Old Maid Marsh. She's— she's froze to death." A dry sob caught in his throat.

There was a general movement toward the cab. They were too late. A gust of wind stirred the unsteady snow. Through the white curtain came the grey-clad Gletha, bearing the immobile body of the tiny woman. The crowd of a dozen or so parted to let them pass. Ear-flapped caps were pulled respectfully from ill-kempt heads.

As Gletha moved toward Aunt Minnie T.'s barren room at the back of the store, Mel Zilitz bustled in to take charge.

"Give her to me, witchlady—and then git. We'll lay her in the shed 'til we can put her away right when spring comes."

Gletha turned a long, penetrating look on him—then stepped into the bedroom. She kicked the door shut behind her. The reverberations from the sharp-edged slam caught the crowd off-guard.

Tom Geddy exploded, "My gawd! That was enough to wake the dead!"

Mel shouted, "Shut up, Tom! Ain't you got no respect?" He escaped the ensuing nervous giggles by arranging and re-arranging boxes of rifle shells on the dusty shelf.

The crowd shuffled toward the ring of chairs around the stove. The waiting silence was broken only by the crackle of peanut shells and the nervous shifting of booted feet on the sawdust-covered floor.

The grandfather clock in the corner tolled high noon with singularly hollow tones. As the final echoes died away, the door to Minnie's room opened. Gletha, the goatlady, stood silhouetted in the bright sunlight pouring through the un-curtained window behind her. The grey cloths clung to her body. Strands of sweat-drenched hair straggled across her face. The men leaped to their feet. With the dignity of an an-cient priestess, she passed through their midst and out the front door. Accompanied by whirling ghosts of light snow, she disappeared.

"Now what are you all standin' there gawkin' about?" The imperious voice of Aunt Minnie T. whirled them around like gigantic fear-filled puppets suspended on wires. Aunt Min-nie T. stood in the doorway, backed by the intense gold of the westering sun flaming through the bare window.

Tom Geddy stammered, "But-but-but—you're dead! I pulled you out of your car myself. You were stiff as a board...froze plumb solid!"

"Now that's the stupidest story I ever heard—amongst all the stupid stories I hear you fellahs tell. I just fell asleep at the wheel and Gletha came along and found me and carried me home and woke me up. Me—dead? Nonsense! But there's gonna' be some dead folks around here if you don't all clear out long enough for me to rid up this place. Now git—all of you!"

The men walked silently back to their tarpaper shacks in nearby forest clearings. Some re-joined their wives and children, touching them with unaccustomed tenderness after their experience in Bear Run Store. Nobody noticed the grey shape at the timber's edge watching Aunt Minnie T. through the window. Gletha, the goatlady, appeared to be leaning, ex-hausted, on golden light.

The Sobbing Stone

"Are you gonna' remember the next time, kid?"

The freshly skinned birch branch whistled through the air, leaving an angry welt on my naked buttock. I clenched my teeth harder, determined not to give my raging father the benefit of the scream of pain gathering in my gut. Deep inside me I hungered for another daddy who might hold me close instead of giving me the ceaseless whippings.

Once again I'd "forgotten" to follow through completely on an assigned task. Disaster had ensued. Now I was paying the price.

One day Dad came home with a little gasoline engine and the necessary apparatus for mounting it on the barnyard pump. No longer would we have to spend hours pumping water into two oak tanks for the livestock. The wondrous engine would do it for us—but it had to be carefully watched. In the midst of our constant poverty, I was never sure whence the money for it came.

The light was scarcely breaking when my father left our shack to join the lumberjacks who lived in the bunkhouse just north of our farmstead. The summer had been unusually dry. Crops would not amount to much. The large garden's produce was slim. My mother worried that the cellar would not be full of home-canned fruits and vegetables for winter. Dad decided to spend some days cutting timber in order to save a little money to supplement our nearly non-existent income.

I was sitting on a stump at the edge of our browning alfalfa field. I watched as the distant fawns jumped stiff-legged in blissful freedom. Near at hand, the lambs frolicked in the same rhythms and patterns behind the woven-wire fence. I, who seldom played, lost myself in their parallel games. The moment was shattered by the shack's screen door slamming with unusual vigor. Dad's voice had a harsh edge: "Git off yer butt, kid, and git the livestock watered. Fill both tanks. Remember, the water level in the well is real low, so don't take your eyes off the motor. Otherwise the pressure will pull sand into the pipe and clog it."

He turned from me abruptly and strode into the woods, the first rays of the sun glinting on the double-bitted ax he carried easily on his shoulder.

My mother stepped into the yard. Her voice hovered on the edge of tears as she said, "He slammed the door double-hard for no reason. The darkness is building up inside him again. He's gonna' move into it. Walk softly around him and do as he says."

She headed toward the scraggly garden to pick some peas before the dew dried. Custom had it that they kept better if you got them early.

My mother always called the periods of silent terror into which my father sank his darknesses. Much of the time he was tender, laughing, outgoing. He'd do anything for anybody. The neighbors saw only that side of him. During our days and nights of fear we kept him hidden. It was shameful to be "sick in the head." As he was about to enter those caves of black anger, he'd beat us both at the slightest provocation. Then he'd sit for days with his head in his hands. Sometimes his cheeks would run with silent tears.

Mom knelt in the garden to pick the scanty pods, a kitchen Madonna in a feedsack dress patterned with fading water lilies in stark contrast to the parched earth. She seemed to be making supplication for a more bounteous harvest to an as yet unhearing deity.

Skip, my black and white mongrel dog, shoved a stick into my hand. I tossed it toward the barnyard. He retrieved it with the grace of a prize setter. We gamed our way to the well. I poured a bit of water down the pump to prime it and started the little engine. I watched in momentary wonder as it moved the proper pulleys and relieved me of the shoulder-wrenching task of working the pump handle for endless hours.

As the water rose within tongue-reach, the team of worn plowhorses and eleven Holstein milk cows competed for space around the edge of the larger of the two moss-covered tanks. The sheep waited patiently until I switched the trough from the pump to their lower tank. It was still running full, as if the water would flow forever.

Far in the woods to the south I heard Skip yelp again and again in dire pain. The sound changed to a steady barking charged with frantic anger. I knew immediately what had happened. I turned from stewarding the running water and rushed to my father's workshed. I grabbed a pair of long-nosed pliers. Skip's cries quickly drew me deep into the forest.

The porcupine crouched motionless on a pine branch, tantalizingly close to the leaping, baying dog. Skip's mouth bristled with quills of varying lengths. He had surprised the little beast on the ground. Sensing danger, the porcupine had fanned out its defense mechanism just as the dog grabbed. This scene had happened many times before.

Upon seeing me, the dog became suddenly silent. He crouched guiltily on the thick brown carpet of pine needles. I knelt at his side. He snuggled up against me. I stammered in disgust, "Ski-Ski-Skippy, will you n-n-never learn?"

We were in for a long session. One by one I gripped the quills with the pliers and gave a quick jerk. Skip suffered silently.

I don't know how long I was involved in the task of mercy when Skip stiffened and gave a low warning growl. I spun around, expecting to confront a timber denizen. Instead, I found myself face-to-face with my father.

He had one arm looped through the bail of an empty half-gallon Karo Syrup bucket. It looked like he might have decided to quit logging early and go blueberry picking. His face, a distorted mask of anger, belied that impression.

He was trimming a freshly cut birch switch with his jackknife. Suddenly, the slant of the sun told me it was early afternoon. I had been gone for hours, forgetting the running water.

Under such circumstances he usually beat me down first with a gust of profanity. At the moment, however, he stared at me in silence. Skippy crept away into the underbrush. I wished Daddy'd swear, but the only sound was the gentle swish of the knife as it cut away twigs and bark, shaping a moist, supple instrument of punishment.

His first strained words were, "Kid, will you never learn? You're always kitin' around the woods with either that damned dog or that crazy old witchlady. I came out of the timber for lunch and found the tank overflowed. The barnyard looks like the Great Bog. The stock can't drink without goin' knee-deep in mud. They'll all get hoof rot. The worst of it is the well ran dry and the flow pipe's clogged with sand. I don't know where we're goin' to find the money to have the well-rigger come and blow it out. If your ma'd had the wax out of her ears, she might have heard the pump gaspin' and saved one piece of your hide. I heard your dog raisin' a fuss earlier in the morning, so I knew where to find you and didn't have to guess much to know what happened."

As he spoke, he continued to hone the switch to cruel perfection. His accusing eyes held mine in an angry grasp. There was a long silence. It was finally broken by two sounds: the click of the jackknife blade as my father finished his disciplinary preparations and the gentle swish of the porcupine's quills. Not wishing to witness what was to come it slithered down the tree and into the bushes.

He addressed an unexpected question to me: "How old are you, kid?"

"N-n-nine," I stammered. As the beatings intensified over the years, the stammer followed suit.

"Nine what?"

"N-n-nine...Sir."

"Well, good. I'm just gonna' give you nine little reminders that will sharpen your memory the next time. Turn around and drop 'em!"

My summer attire consisted only of bib overalls and heavy high-top work shoes. I turned away from him. My hands were shaking as I tried to release a suspender clasp. He stepped forward, tore the suspenders from my shoulders and, shucking me bare as an ear of sweet corn, tossed the protective denim over the pine branch which had been the porcupine's refuge. He threw the Karo bucket into the midst of a patch of blueberries off to my right.

I waited for the first blow to fall. A jay screamed from the top of an oak tree. I heard the slow "thwack" of the switch as Dad softly slapped the palm of his left hand. He was winding up his strength—and my fear. I closed my eyes tightly. SLASH! The blow was unerringly centered on the soft flesh between my neck and left shoulder. Light seemed to explode behind my eyelids. Long moments passed. SLASH! The corresponding spot on the right was similarly marked. With each blow the jay screamed, allowing me to keep my teeth tightly clenched. SLASH! The center of my back bore a long, violent autograph.

"Are you gonna' remember the next time, kid?"

SLASH! The freshly skinned birch branch whistled through the air, leaving an angry welt on my naked left buttock. SLASH! He quickly established a parallel pattern on the right.

Interminable moments passed. I hoped that he had relented and would be satisfied with five reminders. A dry twig snapped behind me. I glanced over my shoulder to see that he had merely changed positions and was eying my lower regions appraisingly. I turned my head away quickly and closed my eyes again. Simultaneously the switch was propelled expertly upward. The crack between my buttocks caught fire. The tip of the switch, softened by repeated use, nicked the back of my scrotum like a hot match tip. My testicles retracted in stark terror.

SLASH! SLASH! SLASH! Three final, rapid horizontal blows marked thighs, backs of knees and calves.

He was breathing hard from exertion. He managed to gasp out, "Now, git yer butt over to that blueberry patch. I don't want to see your good-for-nothin' face at the house until the bucket's full. You can sell them on the roadside to help pay for the well repair. Now, let's see how fast you can move, or I'll turn you around and give you one last reminder where it really hurts."

My hands fell protectively to my privates. I crouched, unable to move. I don't know how long I balanced there, frozen, semi-conscious in a standing fetal position. I was brought back to the present by a light object striking my head and falling to the ground at my feet. The now silent jay had settled on a branch above me. He had gifted me with an acorn to let me know that I did not have to face the next moments friendless. I looked around for my father. He had faded away as noiselessly as a woodland beast.

I reached for my overalls. The mere touch of the fabric to my lacerated body was agony. The suspenders exactly matched the birch tattoos on my shoulders. I dropped them quickly for the second time in the last half-hour.

The day was hot, the kind of heat which penetrates even the deepest forest shadows and transforms them into witches' ovens. As I squatted naked, listening to the dull ping of berries beginning to cover the bottom of the bucket, sweat ran down my back. The salt made the wounds flame.

Finishing the patch to which I had been directed by my father, I moved through the dappled glades carrying my clothing, syrup pail in hand, searching for the furtive blueberries. I knew I did not dare appear at home without the bucket overflowing. I also knew that it would be dark before I found satisfactory quantities of the tiny berries.

Then I heard it: the sighing—the sad song of the wind in the trees, though there was no wind. I followed the sound through what seemed to be an impenetrable barrier of thorn bushes and found myself at the edge of a barren hillside covered with granite outcroppings. The sound came from the stones themselves.

The shaven hairs on the back of my nine-year-old neck crawled across my skin like a giant caterpillar. All the nightmare terrors that ever haunted my swirling dreams climaxed in this daylit moment: the very stones were crying.

I stood at the edge of the clearing, ready to bolt. Then it moved—the most misshapen of the rocks. Foot lifted to flee, I was halted in the awkward pose of escape by the knowledge of just what I was observing.

It was Gletha.

Torn between flight and the sound of her sobs, I stood at the clearing's edge. The great head turned. The eyes caught mine—and held them. How many times would those wells of darkness draw me to do the unwanted. Between gasps that seemed torn from her soul, she called: "Rogee, come quick. I need you." The desire to flee was overwhelming—but the eyes and the sound drew me.

I dropped my nearly empty bucket and my overalls and clambered cautiously over the knife-sharp rocks. It seemed to make no difference that I was naked. She had seen the scarred nakedness of my heart so many times that the bareness of my body fell into proper perspective. Reaching her, I noticed a full bucket of blueberries at her side. I could not escape her extended arms feathered with her flowing cloths like great wings. She embraced me with a desperate closeness that made me expect the silence of the clearing to be fractured by my cracking ribs. Strangely, her clasp did not exacerbate the wounds from the afternoon. Holding me briefly at arm's length, she blurted out, "Rogee, I had a terrible dream...a terrible dream." I turned my head to avoid the spittle of fear which sprayed my face with every "t." A resolve to break and run for it almost overwhelmed me, but her face, twisted in agony, mesmerized me into staying. She crushed me against her great breasts and sobbed again.

"W-w-w-what scared y-y-you, Gletha?" I managed to stammer out. Gletha never laughed when I tried to talk to her. She'd do a strange thing instead. She'd take her hand and gently stroke my back. In spite of her own fear, she was doing it now. The stammer lessened—as did the pain in my battered body.

"It was the rock in the black sky—the rock in the black sky." Her whole body shuddered as the vision out of sleep returned. "The rock was whirling all by itself way out among the stars—and I was on the rock. I was all by myself—whirling away forever. And there warn't no people—nor no goats—nor no boys or trees or blueberries—just me whirling all by myself in the black sky." Her voice descended to a fear-strained whisper in those final words.

She controlled her sobs for a moment. "I knew there was never no chance to touch nobody again. Never no chance...never no chance." Her despair leveled off into a hopeless chant. I managed to free my arms and almost against my will found myself clutching her tightly in return.

Out of the corner of my eye I saw the sky. It had suddenly

turned as black as the heavens in Gletha's dream. The sun had disappeared completely. There was a hush soon to be truncated by the thunder's voice. "G-G-G-Gletha, w-w-w-we've g-g-got to run for it!"

Perhaps my stammer too long delayed the suggested action. Wind tore at the tall pines. Torrents drenched us instantly. The cold rain further soothed my fevered cuts. Gletha's sobs ceased—only to be replaced by my cry of fear. I knew we were whirling in a roiling, turning world, and I could only confess, "G-G-Gletha, I-I-I'm scared."

She began to sing one of her strange, wild songs. I felt the wear-feathered cloths descend around me, bringing an unearthly warmth. Her hand, toughly tender on a goat's teat or a boy's back, began to move up and down. Enthroned in the midst of the grey field, bits of hail reinforcing the wind and the rain, Gletha began to move to the rhythm of the wind. The wordless song shaped itself more specifically and I heard, "We're a'touching. We're a'touching. Praise the Lord of the storm and the darkness and light, we're a'touching. We're a'touching."

I added without a trace of hesitation, "I'm really glad, Gletha."

When the storm passed, she filled my bucket with her berries. I drew on my soaked overalls. We each headed for our homes—though we had discovered a healing home together on the hillside.

It was night when I stole quietly into our shack, taking care to close the screen door silently. My mother was sitting alone in the kitchen. A kerosene lamp burned dimly in the living room. My father sat in the worn rocking chair, his head in his hands. The lamp would burn through the night. Outer darkness was intolerable to him when he was overcome by the darkness within. The dim light, which spilled over into the kitchen, illumined Mom's blackened left eye. I wished that Gletha, the goatlady, might have stroked her cheek as she had my back. I kissed the bruise and went wordlessly to my bedroom.

I slipped out of my shoes and overalls. I removed a flashlight from its hiding place under my mattress where I kept it for surreptitious reading. I stepped in front of the

Jubilee Celebration of Diocese
2/9/14 Sun. noon
All Sis + Bros also

Tom H. DIANNA 520-229.3276

Museum of Art — Park Ave + Speedway
Tues - Fri, 9 - 5 (NOT Mondays) $5.00

*De Grazia — 10 to 4
Old Tucson

146 N. Main — Tuc Mus of Art (downtown) $8, or $6.
(Closed Mondays) open 10 - 4

Biosphere $20., 9 - 4:00

cracked mirror and shined its beam down my back. The skin bore no marks of my father's devastation.

Healing to Whole

It would not have happened if Brock Munson's prize heifer, Darlene, had not given birth to a three-legged calf. But then, Gletha, the goatlady, would have been blamed, no matter what. If it wasn't for the calf, Old Mel Zilitz would be in his grave right now.

Mel Zilitz thought he was the boss of the whole created world—at least that piece of it surrounding Bear Run Store. When the proprietress of the establishment, Aunt Minnie T., had to be away on family matters, she left Mel in charge. The entire neighborhood prayed for the health of Aunt Minnie's distant relatives.

When Bear Run School let out for the afternoon, the children could always depend on a piece of hard candy one way or another: a few for a penny or a piece out of her ample apron pocket if pennies were in short supply. Sometimes half the classroom would gather around the big potbellied stove, and Aunt Minnie would help with geography lessons or an arithmetic problem. Aunt Theo, who taught the school, always said that Minnie was a born teacher who could take over her classroom anytime she wanted.

It was late November when Aunt Minnie T.'s sister, Abigail, came down sick a hundred miles away in Wolfsville. Sad to say, when word got around about Abigail taking to her bed with dropsy, there was more concern about store management than about the poor lady's health.

Mel Zilitz was the most disagreeable man in Bear Run

Township. It isn't very Christian to put down a person because of his appearance, but he looked like a pocketgopher. The whole countryside was undermined with gopher tunnels. A horse's hoof could drop through into one of their holes and a leg be strained or broken. A deer might snap a leg bone. The county agent let it be known that anybody would be paid a dime for every sun-dried gopher tail turned in at the courthouse in Birch River. All the kids started setting small traps in the tunnels. They didn't greet each other with, "How many gophers did'ja git today?" but rather with, "How many Mels did'ja trap?"

It wasn't just his looks that folk objected to. Whenever Mel was behind the counter and handed anything to customers, he did it in a way that made them feel he was afraid to touch them. Granted, nobody had any running water and baths were weekly, but everybody did their best. People had their pride. Mel always insulted that pride.

He'd been to college for a year. That made him better than anybody else—or so he thought. Folk accused him of "puttin' on airs" when he talked.

He seemed to hate children. As they passed through the store after school, he'd never help them with their homework. When jobs in the timber were scarce for fathers, empty-pocketed children would gather at the glass case which held the wonderworld of penny sweets. There was never any free candy. When it became obvious that sales would not be made, he herded them out roughly: "If you're not purchasing today, it's time to get out from under foot."

At age fifty-five, he was unmarried. He'd worked from job to job. He'd tried employment with Mortician Mackin in Deerville, but the sight of blood made him sick. He'd done odd jobs. Most of the time he cared for his aging mother. When she died two years earlier, word went 'round that "Old Mel Zilitz come into a little money."

After the mythic death of Aunt Minnie T.'s husband Ned in "the worst sawmill accident in the history of Pine Ring County" (as tellers of the tale always began), Mel began to spend more and more time at the store. Some folks said he had "designs" on Aunt Minnie—and her business establishment. Others said "her heart was bigger'n her head." Still others said "she just hankered after a little constant courtin'." There was probably an element of truth in each of these guesses. The moment Aunt Minnie T. was off to care for Abigail, Mel took over the store with a vengeance. He immediately began insulting the customers. Darby Jones had trapped some extra mink. He had more money in his pocket than usual. He allowed Letty, his wife, to come to the store and look for some material for a new dress rather than wait for matching feedsacks from the elevator in Spruce Crossing. Mel hovered. He grasped each bolt of fabric so that Letty could not unroll a few rounds. She wanted to swathe it royally around her shoulders and pose before the full-length mirror with the peeling golden Cupids on the top and the silvering going bad— "just to see how it'd look on me." Mel thought her threadbare winter coat appeared a mite soiled and didn't want his fabric getting too close to it. Letty left without making a choice. Tears marred her strange green eyes.

In spite of the temporary proprietor's treatment of customers, loggers and would-be farmers and road workers from the nearby shacks still would gather 'round the big stove and share their tall tales and carpet the bare, wide-planked floor with peanut shells. Without Aunt Minnie T. present to keep him in line, Mel always had to be the first and the loudest. The sharing time around the potbellied heater was never quite as much fun.

Mel Zilitz hated Gletha, the goatlady. She would look at him deeply when she came to the store to deliver pails of goatmilk which were sold to those who had ulcers and to families with new babies whose mothers could not nurse them. In return, she received flour, sugar, lard, yeast, salt and raisins for her goatmilk pudding. She also received special spices which she couldn't find in the woods: mustard, basil and marjoram used in her healing salves and syrups and poultices. Mel complained to his cronies, "That witchwoman can see right through you with those scary eyes."

Aunt Minnie T. always welcomed Gletha with her milk into the store. They often compared remedies for whatever illness was going around the township or the newest malady to attack Aunt Minnie T.'s sickly relatives.

Mel gave Gletha a different set of orders. As long as he was in charge, she was never to come into the store. She was to leave her Karo Syrup pails of milk on the porch. He'd bring her out what she wanted in exchange. He always tried to give her as little as possible.

It was Old Mel Zilitz who kept alive the persistent rumor that Gletha was a witch. He would skillfully insert a comment into the stove-side conversation such as, "I wonder how that snot-nosed, skinny, stammering boy that hangs around with Gletha can trap more gophers than all the other boys put together? I imagine she brews up some kind of potion to put on his traps that attracts the gophers right into them." Heads would nod in sage agreement as fathers whose sons were far behind in the gopher competition let their jealousy overrun their reason.

The talk would die down for a while. Then something always happened that would bring Gletha's supposed powers of destructive magic to public attention.

This time, it was Brock Munson's tragedy. His heifer, Darlene, had taken the grand prize at Pine Ring County Fair. Everybody in Bear Run Township had been rooting for Brock and Darlene. Everybody felt they had a share in the prize. Folk looked forward to her first offspring so that the triumph might be repeated in next autumn's competition. Darlene, unfortunately, birthed a three-legged calf.

Brock leaned against the Bear Run Store counter paying for shotgun shells. The calf had just been born. Mel Zilitz was the first to know.

Brock shared: "Poor little thing. I was jist sick. Darlene managed to nuzzle it up on its three scrawny legs so's it could nurse—but I don't hold out much hope for it. I could keep it in a pen in the barn for the rest of the spring, but soon's I put it in the pasture the wolves will jist pull the poor little cripple down. Might be the most merciful thing to put a bullet in it's head right now."

Mel offered his nasal, high-pitched sympathy, "I just don't know how such a terrible thing could come out of such a beautiful heifer—a prize-winner at that. Perhaps somebody cast a spell on poor Darlene."

Mel's gopher eyes squinted more than usual as he continued, "Have you had anything to do with Old Lady Gletha the last few months? I understand she can cast some strong curses on man and beast if she's ever crossed."

Brock thought for a long moment as he put the shotgun shells in his pocket. Then he explained, "Mel, I think you may be onto something there. Last summer Gletha and that snot-nosed kid stopped by my house. He'd just beat out my Bonnie in a contest at the Lakeside Church of Jesus Risen. I just knew they'd come by to lord it over us. They didn't mention the contest. Gletha did say they'd found a bee tree on the back part of our place and could they take some of the honey? I got 'em to tell me exactly where it was since I didn't even know it was there. I told 'em they most certainly could not have any since we needed it all ourselves. Then Gletha asked if'n they could collect it on shares. I just told 'em to git off my property. The rest of the summer I'd see 'em like a coupla' shadows hauntin' around my woods diggin' roots and stuff. I'd chase 'em off. A few days later I'd see 'em ag'in."

Mel zeroed in on a bit of Gospel truth: "Brock, you have your answer right there. The witchwoman put a spell on Darlene to get even with you. What more proof do you need?"

Brock paused in silent wonder at Mel's insight. He responded, "I gotta' thank yuh, Mel, fer puttin' me on the right track. After they told me where it wuz, I put on my honey hat with the nettin' and my gloves and my extra-heavy pants. Now, I've bin takin' honey from bee trees all my life and am seldom ever stung. But them bees wuz wild! They found ways to git at me I'd never been gotten at before. They was up my pantlegs and down my shirt before I'd knowed what hit me. I had to take to my bed fer three days. I couldn't stand no clothes near to me and Nell had to pack the stings with blue mud. Yunno' what I bet happened, Mel? That miserable witch-woman put a curse on poor Darlene! One of these days I'm gonna' take a shot at her." He fingered the shells in his pocket.

When the regulars gathered around the stove, Mel planted the story of the terrible curse—replete with the tale-teller's special details: "Brock saw Old Witch Gletha and that boy standing in the cowyard in the moonlight scattering something on Darlene," and "Now I'm telling you, those were not ordinary bees. They were huge. Each one had a red cross on her back."

The narrative of events surrounding the tragic birth of the three-legged calf was told and retold throughout the neighborhood. It was enhanced by each teller's particular point of view. The suspicions were entrenched. What more proof did anyone need that the mysterious woman was a confirmed witch? All the fears that anyone had about anything could be nicely concentrated in the single figure of Gletha, the goatlady.

Aunt Minnie T. sent word that Abigail was worsening. Her days away stretched into weeks. Mel Zilitz's rule at Bear Run Store became more firm.

In early March, an unexpected thaw surprised the countryside. Roads buckled from frost heaves. As the snow melted, the unpaved parking lot became swamp-like. The men in the neighborhood gathered on the store's wide porch to marvel at the weather. They were careful not to lean against the decaying poplar pole-railings. Some of them moved inside to sit around the stove for perhaps the last time of the winter. They ate peanuts and swapped lies.

Mel remained enthroned on his stool behind the till. From this vantage point he could watch the merchandise throughout the entire store. He always sought to confirm his basic suspicion: anyone entering carried the potential to "steal me blind." The till was also out of the way of drafts so that Mel could protect himself from anything which might worsen the "usual touch of spring cold on my lungs."

Cripple-Clive Marsden saw us coming: Gletha, the goatlady, her soft grey cloths flowing in the light breeze, a pail of milk in each hand, followed by me. We picked our way carefully through the muddy ruts.

Cripple-Clive let out a holler, "Mel, the old witchlady and that snot-nosed kid's comin'."

Mel finished making change for Clete Roberts' snuff. He quickly made his way through the stove-side crowd and headed toward the front door. Seeing no one to apprehend us, Gletha and I had quietly climbed the rickety steps all the way up onto the porch. Mel confronted us just outside the door.

"Listen here, old lady. How many times have I told you not to come up to this door. You just leave your milk on the porch and be on your way—both of you!"

Gletha looked at him out of those steady pools of darkness. She did something she'd never done before. As if to affirm her rightful place in the community, she stepped toward Mel, planning to walk around him and enter the store like any other neighborhood woman. He shifted his weight slightly and shot out a hand to stop her. He hit her shoulder, catching her off balance. She swayed backwards. I tried to catch her. It was too late. She struck a decaying pole in the porch railing. It snapped—a sickening sound, like the crack of a horse's leg plunging into a gopher hole. Gletha plummeted five feet down off the porch and landed with a muffled thud in the soft spring mud. She lay motionless for a long moment. The onlookers heard the splintering rail. They rushed to the porch, clustering around Mel. There were scattered guffaws—and then a strange, waiting silence.

Gletha seemed not so much to lift herself out of the mud as to flow gracefully upwards. Her eyes caught Mel Zilitz's and held them. The grey cloths clung to her. She looked like a clay sculpture of an ancient prophetess.

The group on the porch edged backward before the force of her stare. Then, without a word, she turned and wrapped the end of a mud-stained soft grey cloth around my shoulders. She took my hand. Together, we glided across the parking lot and disappeared into the forest.

Mel pushed through the crowd and sought the safety of his stool and cash register. The conversation boiled around him. It was summarized by Cook Tom from the lumber camp: "Mel, yuh shoulbna' done that. The witchwoman will hunt yuh 'n curse yuh the rest of yer days!"

Mel responded angrily, "Now, you just stop that kind of talk. I really want to clear this store. I have a lot of shelf-stocking to do, and you'll just be in my way."

The men reluctantly moved toward the door. Mel could not help overhearing their sniggering comments: "Did'ja see them two fly into the woods when they left? Ol' Mel is gonna' get his now. Next time we see him he'll prob'ly have blue ears or two noses or be missin' some vitals between his legs." Raw laughter echoed through the pines.

Mel locked the front door behind him. He turned the CLOSED sign to the outside and pulled down the window shades. He stood in the semi-darkness, feeling terror well up inside him.

Three weeks passed. The weather took a sudden turn into a severe, late-spring blizzard. Visibility was zero as the wind churned the powder-dry snow into great drifts. During a brief lull in the storm, I struggled through the butt-deep snow to Gletha and Pud's shack. I was escaping a destructive outburst from my father, whose depression deepened with the rising drifts. As I opened the warped storm door, I was nearly overcome by the smell of herbs cooking on the woodstove. Gletha was making salve. She motioned me silently to the table. I knew my job. I picked up the pestle and began to crush strange herbs in the stone bowl that looked like it might have belonged to a Druid in King Arthur's time. From a stone crock on a shelf, Gletha poured some goat-milk into a pan. She added a generous dollop of Karo Syrup. She heated it while she continued to stir the salve. After a few moments, she poured milk and Karo into a battered tin cup and set it in front of me as I sat shivering at the table.

The only sounds were the wind, which had chillingly intensified, the gentle boil of the herb-laced liquid and the rhythmic snores of the sleeping Pud. Weaving the sounds together was the wordless chant which Gletha breathed as she stirred.

The scene was shattered by the bell of the telephone on the wall. I automatically leapt to my feet, scampered across the room, eased the receiver off the hook and covered the mouthpiece with my other hand. Gletha stared disapprovingly at my rubbernecking, that illicit listening to party-line conversations which was a major form of recreation during the dull winter days.

The call was being put through to my cousin, Mildred. The voice was barely understandable. After a moment, I recognized the caller as Mel Zilitz.

Mel was gasping for breath after nearly every word: "Mildred—I'm terribly sick. My fever's almost 105 and I can hardly breathe. Aunt Minnie T.'s still with her sister Abigail, and the storm is too bad to summon the doctor from Birch River."

He paused as a round of coughing tore at him. There was

silence for a moment. Then he gasped, "Mildred, I must have some help. I've taken everything in the store that's supposed to soothe some part of my sickness. Nothing does. What am I going to do?"

She responded helplessly, "Mel, I jist dunno'. Ain't no way we kin git to you from way up here at the far end of the township. Yuh can't see a thing outside. I guess iff'n I was you, I'd call Gletha to see if there's anything she's got that might help."

I stiffened. Gletha help him? After what Mel Zilitz had done to her? No way!

There was a long silence on the telephone. Then Mel gasped out, "I can't call her, Mildred. I knocked her off the store porch. I'm sure it's one of her spells that's clogged my chest."

Mildred exploded, "Don't be a fool, Mel. I thought you'd bin to college. Yuh prob'ly got the pneumonia. Yuh either call her or die there in yer own juices!"

I slammed the receiver into its cradle on the side of the phone. I spun on Gletha. My words tumbled out angrily, "That was Old Mel Zilitz talkin' to Mildred. He's terrible sick and can't get a doctor and he's going to call you and after what he did to you don't you even answer the phone and don't you go near him and just let him die which is what he deserves."

Gletha looked hard at me, stopping the flow of words. "You quiet your mouth, boy. He's a destroyer, that man, but somewhere down inside him is the image of God which nobody's maybe ever looked deep enough to find. If a living thing is hurting, you try to heal it whole again—no matter what the past has brought."

She had scarcely finished her words when the telephone rang a second time. Two long rings were easily identifiable as Gletha and Pud's signal. She moved toward the phone, removed the receiver and spoke a single, low-voiced word into the mouthpiece: "Yes?"

The batteries in the phone were nearly new. Standing across the room I could hear Mel coughing into the receiver. Gletha listened to him pleading for her to come. There was a long silence. Mel reached the end of his strength. She hung up the receiver without saying a word.

I was jubilant. "You've changed yer mind, haven't yuh? Yer

gonna' let Old Gopher Mel cough hisself into the lake of fire, aren't yuh?"

She stared at me, shook her head sadly and said, "You don't hear so good, do you?" From the top shelf, she reached down a mason jar of powdered herbs. She poured more goatmilk into the pan, sprinkling it with some herbs from the jar. She reached toward one of the many bunches of dried plants hanging upside-down from the shack's bare rafters. Breaking off a piece which retained a deep purple color, she handed it to me for grinding. I picked up the pestle and ground a couple of turns. I wrinkled my nose and spoke through an impending sneeze, "This junk smells like ground stinkbug, Gletha. Whatever it is I'm grindin' ought to kill him for sure."

Gletha added the fresh-ground, vile-smelling herb to the warming milk. When the boiling concoction was cooked to her satisfaction, she poured it into a Karo Syrup pail.

Standing by the window, I said, "Gletha, it's gittin' dark and the snow's blowin' so bad that nobody can see nothin', and so there's no way we can git to Bear Run Store—even if Ol' Mel Zilitz were the nicest guy in the world, which he ain't."

Gletha simply motioned to my sheepskin coat hanging on the back of a chair. She wrapped some extra layers of the soft grey cloth around herself as I shrugged my way into the coat and put on my wool cap and horsehide gloves. We stepped out into the storm, carrying the pail with the milk and a tin of the freshly made salve. It felt as if we were floating on the gusts of the storm.

In an incredibly brief time, the peeling hulk of Bear Run Store loomed out of the swirling snow. Gletha and I waded up the unshoveled steps, feeling strangely free. We were going to open the door and walk through the store to Mel's room in the rear. Nobody was going to stop us.

The door to the untidy quarters was open. Mel was stretched out on his cot, exhausted from his telephonic efforts. Sweat was pouring down his face. The only sounds were the howling wind and the bone-dry rattle in his chest.

Kneeling by his bedside, Gletha picked up a tablespoon that Mel had obviously been using to take some patent medicine. The empty bottle stood on the orange crate by the bed. Its marvelous promise of cures for every disease known to man or beast stood out in large letters readable even in the dim illumination through the heavily smoked globe of the kerosene lamp which Mel had managed to light. Using the spoon handle, she pried the lid off the pail. Grasping the sides of his jaw with her left hand, she forced open his mouth and spooned into it some of the vile-tasting herbs and milk. The death-mask face began to wrinkle. When the full force of the herbs took effect, his throat convulsed and his whole body gave a jerk. Then he relaxed. He still did not open his eyes. Gletha unscrewed the lid from the tin of salve. Pulling back the soiled quilt and lifting Mel's threadbare flannel shirt, she began gently rubbing the salve across his bony chest. Its pleasant odor was a welcome contrast to the nauseous smell of the milk and herbs. His breathing calmed as she stroked him. Mel opened his eyes. He stared at the kneeling woman. In the light of the kerosene lamp, I thought I saw tears glistening on the detested man's sharp-boned cheeks. It was amazing how that bit of moisture made Old Mel Zilitz seem less gopher-like. He closed his eyes again. Gletha motioned to me. Mel was breathing quietly. He seemed to be in a deep sleep. We eased the lamp's wick down until the light was out, walked through the darkened store and softly closed the heavy front door. Swathed in the soft grey cloths, we floated through the wind-whipped snow to the pungent warmth of Gletha's shack.

The storm abated in the night. I returned to Bear Run Store in the morning sunlight, carrying a can of goatmilk sweetened with a touch of Karo Syrup.

I found Mel wrapped in a worn, dirty patchwork comforter. He was sitting in a rocking chair by the potbellied stove which he had managed to coax into intense warmth. Mel said, "You were here with Gletha last night, weren't you?"

Placing the still-warm milk on the table at Mel's side, I admitted my presence.

"I think you probably saved my life."

"Not m-m-me! 'Twas her, Gletha, the g-goatlady, who you knocked in the mud. And let me tell you, Mel Zilitz, iff'n it had been me what made the decision to stay or come last night, you'd be dead now! But Gletha fixed the herbs and milk and salves, sayin' somethin' about an image of God inside you where nobody'd ever looked hard enough to find it—and that if anybody hurts, you gotta' heal 'em, no matter what they've done. Well, let me tell you, the only image o' God I know anything about is the one you knocked into the mud."

I was crying. I ran toward the heavy front door. Mel Zilitz called out, "Wait!"

I turned and, poised for flight, stared at Mel as he continued, "I've knocked myself and everybody else in the mud for years. I think it's time for all of us to try to help each other out—together."

When Aunt Minnie T. walked into the store four days later, she discovered Gletha, the goatlady, standing at the counter—*inside* the store. She was receiving lard and raisins in bountiful exchange for her milk—straight from the hand of Old Mel Zilitz himself.

The Rose O' Love

I heard the sharp "flip-flop" of her felt slippers which never came up over her heels. Looking out the window, I saw Cousin Florrie marching authoritatively along the parched gravel road. The offending footwear smoked up the thick, soft dust. She appeared to be striding through the fire of righteousness itself.

She burst through the door of our shack and slammed herself into a chair at the quilting frame. She had been preceded by two other ladies. Her face was a mask of condemnation as she emitted a heavy sigh and thundered out her latest news of disaster.

"That ugly little Calley Harris is going to marry Peter Stopes, and I think it's positively shameful for her to accept his proposal since she don't own a quilt to her name."

Tongues clucked in agreement. Needles continued to compete as to who could make the smallest stitches in the "Dresden Plate" quilt nearing completion. Nobody was impolite enough to mention that a cause for Florrie's disgruntlement might well be the fact that she'd hoped for months that Peter would give some attention to her straw-headed daughter, Amantha Sue. However, if Amantha Sue even looked at him, he fled for the forest.

After two hours the finished product was removed from the frame. Each woman admired her handiwork within the community project. Each attested to the fact that it was well-nigh the prettiest quilt they'd ever seen.

Mom laid out angel food cake and coffee. Bethie Wetherford insisted, as usual, that all she could possibly eat was a tiny sliver. Mom gave her half the amount of the others' portions. After a dainty nibble she exclaimed, "I declare, Mary, you make the lightest angel food in Bear Run Township. I guess I'm going to have a regular-size piece after all."

Mom doled her out a second piece, thereby giving her considerably more than anyone else gathered at the crude pine table. This fact was not lost upon the other quilters.

The conversation turned to the strange life of Calley Harris. Florrie provided the intimate details since she'd heard them directly from her mother-in-law, Aunt Jennie Mauldin, who was one of the principle players in the tragic saga.

The Harris cabin was far back on the gently sloping hill rather grandiosely named Pine Mountain. When Calley was prematurely born, her mother died. The Harrises always kept to themselves. Nobody had known Elvira was even pregnant.

When Emil Harris came down from cutting pulpwood on the mountain, he found her already advanced in labor. There was no time to fetch a distant neighbor. He assisted in the birth. He sponged off his new-born daughter, wrapped her in pieces of soft flannel and placed her in the arms of his exhausted wife.

Weeks before, they'd agreed to name the baby Calley if it was a girl. Elvira wanted her deceased mother's name continued in the family.

Elvira assured him she would be fine while he went to the barn to finish the chores. He knelt by the bed and circled them with his arms, laying his rough cheek against his wife's.

He whispered, "Calley's such a beautiful name. I have such a beautiful wife. I know the three of us are going to be happy forever."

Mother and daughter slept deeply. He tiptoed from the room and headed for the barn.

As he returned across the clearing with pails of warm milk, the great wolves howled incessantly. He shivered.

Entering the house, he heard a tiny piercing cry. He removed his screaming daughter from Elvira's now-lifeless arms. He quickly felt for pulse in his wife's wrist and held a mirror to her paling lips. No flow of blood or breath was evident.

The rhythm of sobs tearing his body quieted the child. He stumbled into the small kitchen where he'd left the foaming buckets. He filled a little dish with the still-warm milk. He sat in the rocking chair. He dipped his finger into the liquid and placed on the infant's lips the drops which formed. Both milk and finger were embraced by her suckling lips. Again and again throughout the hours which followed he fed her.

Early the following morning he awoke with a start and discovered that he'd held the child all night. Her eyes were open. She seemed to smile.

Emil lined a wooden peach crate with flannel. Having been placed in her new surroundings, she slept at once.

While finishing the morning chores, he shaped a plan. Aunt Jennie Mauldin's oldest unmarried daughter, Tressa, had become pregnant. Her lover disappeared. In her despair, she killed herself with her father's deer rifle. Perhaps Jennie could work on her grief by helping him with the baby until Calley was old enough to live with him in his remote cabin.

Jennie readily consented. He left the infant with her.

Emil returned to his farmstead. He dug a deep grave in a little glen surrounded by great oaks. He cut some soft cedar boughs and laid them nearby. He carried some slabs from his portable sawmill and placed them by the side of the grave. He framed the excavation and stretched two heavy ropes across the hole. He pounded together a rough coffin and struggled it into position on the ropes. He lined it with the fresh-cut boughs.

Darkness had fallen. A cold moon lighted the glen.

He returned to the house and gently picked up the fragile body of his wife. He processed her through the moonlight and placed her on the soft boughs in the bark-covered box. The night was cold. Emil paused to look at her one last time—then nailed four wide slabs over the top.

He loosened a rope from the frame, lowered a corner of the coffin, then rewound the rope. He stolidly circled the bier, repeating the action at each corner until the box touched the layer of rocks with which he had lined the bottom of the grave. He flicked the ropes atop the coffin.

Sobbing, he placed a layer of large rocks on the coffin lid. Then he filled the cavity with soft earth. In the distance, the great wolves howled a requiem to the pale moon.

For the next five years Emil would appear a time or two a week and snuggle the baby, assist her with her first steps and take her into the woods to show her the nests and dams and caves where life was sheltered beneath the trees.

During those times when Jennie couldn't keep her, Gletha, the goatlady, would take the tiny shadow-creature and teach her the ways of the loon and the firefly.

When she was six, Emil took her back to his distant shack with only rare visits to Jennie and Gletha. Now and then she'd appear for a few days at Bear Run School—just long enough to learn her letters and numbers. She sat in a corner and wouldn't speak to any of the other children. They gaped at her in awe of her strangeness.

She was terribly frail. Her face was narrow and gaunt. Her teeth had come in terribly twisted. She struggled to keep her lips closed. Consequently, she seldom spoke or smiled. Her dark hair was long and coarse. Her feedsack dresses were always faded. But her eyes overcame all her other features. They were beautiful: the vibrant brown of a doe's eyes in sunlight.

It was her eyes that captured Peter Stopes. He was nearly as shy as she was—in stark contrast to his four older brothers who were boisterous to the point of brutality.

The Stopeses lived right next door to Florrie, who described to the assembled quilters in lurid detail how Peter would "shamefacedly sneak off on long courting trips to the far reaches of Pine Mountain."

In a hoarse whisper which she hoped I would not hear, she speculated, "I wouldn't be at all surprised if he hasn't gotten her in a family way."

At that, everyone affirmed that they'd all better get home and gather the eggs and feed the chickens and get something started toward supper.

Marguerite Matson announced, "It's my turn to have the help of all of you. We'll gather at my place next Thursday and begin putting together my 'Star of Texas.' "

After her guests had left, mother sat for a long time in

silence, fondling the Dresden Plate quilt. Then she turned to me and asked, "Roger, do you know where the Harris cabin is back on Pine Mountain?"

I replied, "N-n-no, I don't really. But Gletha does. She and I have been there a time or two, b-b-but I'd get lost goin' by myself."

"Then, walk across the clearing and fetch Gletha."

I was startled into action by this unusual request. I plummeted across the field and burst into her shack. "G-g-g-gletha, c-c-come q-q-q-quick. Ma needs you right away."

She was in the midst of a song-surrounded meditation. My outburst startled her to her feet. "What's the matter? Is Mary hurt? Did your daddy beat her bad again?"

"Naw, she's not hurt. She j-j-just wants to see you right away."

Gletha spoke with unusual sharpness. "Boy, when are you going to learn to move through some moments of life with a little common quietness? Yer always makin' out that every whisper of the wind in the leaves is a crisis."

In spite of her reprimand, she was moving toward the door, adjusting her soft grey garments as she went. The light wind seemed to carry us over the field at near levitation.

Arriving at our house, Mom greeted her warmly. In anticipation of Gletha's appearing, she'd laid out a piece of her famous angel food cake, a bowl of home-canned blueberries, some fresh-baked bread and butter and a mug of steaming coffee.

When we entered, my mother simply said, "Rest yerself. I've set out a little lunch for you."

Gletha sat down. She looked at my mother who had returned to caressing the newly-finished piece of quiltmaker's art. She said, "I feel goodness growing here. What do you need of me, Mary?"

"Florrie was going on about how Peter Stopes was going to marry Calley Harris and about how he'd probably got her pregnant and how she shouldn't be getting married no matter what 'cause she ain't got a quilt to her name. Well, here's what I want you to do. I want you to take this quilt to Pine Mountain. Give it to Calley. Tell her I don't want no folks feelin' she shouldn't get married. Tell her that it's a loan of love. She can give it back if she likes after she gets one done fer herself, but she don't need to feel no push to ever return it."

I was sitting at the table with Gletha. I was running my finger over the near-empty cake plate, drawing pictures in the moist brown crumbs that ever remained after a piece was served. My finger would gather a clump of the delicacy, rich with Watkins' Imitation Vanilla, and when I thought no one was looking, I'd pop it into my mouth.

My mother stood up, put the quilt on the chair by Gletha and put her hands on my shoulders. She said, "Why don't you take this boy with you. His terrible manners have been getting on my nerves lately."

Without touching her food, Gletha floated to her feet and tented us both in a warm embrace.

Gletha picked up the quilt and pulled me to my feet. I was still lost in the spiderweb-like cloth. Mom reached out a hand to the quilt for a final touch. It was not so much that she was reluctant to part with it, but rather she wanted something of her caring to go with it. Both women had tears coursing down their cheeks. I couldn't understand why they were crying over a quilt—but then there were lots of things I didn't much understand.

Gletha secured the quilt somewhere beneath the folds of her soft grey cloths. We floated through the forest to Pine Mountain.

As we neared the Harris' cabin, we heard the rhythm of hard lye soap against a washboard. We knew that clothes were being washed in the oak tub by the back door. We approached silently. The frail sixteen-year-old was so intent on a pair of her dad's overalls, stained with pine sap from his logging trade, that she did not hear us coming.

Steam was rising from the water. Her usually ashen face was flushed. She raised her head to brush the straight hair from her eyes. She saw us and automatically turned to flee, stopped only by a gentle word from Gletha: "Calley."

The girl stopped and responded: "I knew it was you all the time, Gletha—but folks don't never come here. I guess I just always set to run like a fox in the woods. What in the world brings you and Rogee out this way?"

My body tensed. I was about to lash out at her for the use of that hated name when Gletha's gentle touch on my shoulder became a reprimanding talon.

Wiping her soapy hands on the hem of her feedsack dress, she stepped closer to us as Gletha explained our mission: "Florrie told the quilters that you and Peter were going to get married and that you weren't really ready for such a thing when you don't have a quilt of your own to your name."

Gletha dislodged the quilt from the flowing drapes and held it out toward Calley like a queen bestowing great riches. She explained, "The women finished quilting this for Mary. She said she wanted you and Peter to have it."

Calley gasped. She reached out to touch the royal gift, her eyes alive with excitement.

Then her face clouded. She clasped her hands firmly behind her back. "Tell Mary I'm real touched. But I can't possibly take it. Peter has talked a lot about how we just don't want to be beholden to anybody."

Gletha replied, "Calley, when something's offered from the heart, it doesn't mean that you're beholden. Look on it as a loan of love. You can return it when you finish one for yerself. However, when I think of what you've probably got to do to set up housekeeping, that may be a while."

Calley hesitated for a moment. "There's no way it will be new and fresh and as beautiful as it is now when I return it."

"Calley, you got a lot to learn about what makes things beautiful. Knowing it sheltered the two of you will make it even more beautiful to Mary."

I piped up, "Yeah, and Ma's f-f-feelings will be real hurt if you d-d-d-don't take it."

My mouth was encased in a rough hand still redolent with the rich odor of the morning milking. Anger rose in me until I realized that my outburst might make Calley beholden in another way.

She stepped forward, closed her eyes and, blinded by the wonder of the gift, ran her fingers over the minuscule stitches (except for those of Bethie Wetherford which Florrie always judged as being a little clumsy). Then she turned and danced her way into the cabin, whirling with joy, her face buried in the quilt.

No further words were necessary. We turned and made our way lightly through the woods. Gletha sang a song to the sunlit sky. A vee of Canadian honkers passing overhead made antiphonal response.

It had been a night in late August when Peter asked Calley to marry him. They talked far into the night about plans and dreams and when it should all happen. She thought December would be nice. It would give them time to "do everything to start out with."

Peter shared their wedding plans with Phil, his silent father—who shared them with Zora, his wife—who shared them with Florrie, her only confidant—who shared them with anybody who'd listen—especially the Thursday quilters.

The times were hard. Money was scarce. Peter cut pulpwood part-time and worked a full shift in Bill Parson's nearby sawmill. Marrying Calley meant that he could build a little three-room slab-and-tarpaper cabin on the back field of his folks' place and move out of the lumberjacks' bunkhouse where, at his dad's suggestion, he'd moved to "grow up a little."

For the rest of the summer and fall he felled trees on Emil Harris' back acreage. In spite of his not wanting to be beholden to anyone, he allowed his family and a few neighbors to help him saw lumber for the studdings. Soon, the clear outline of three tiny rooms was evident in the forest clearing.

At first, Calley had balked at the thought of moving close to the developed neighborhood around Bear Run Store. Peter assured her that "we can keep to ourselves just as much as we want."

After the arrival of the quilt—which Calley hid from Peter in an old leatherbound trunk—she grew more confident in the presence of folks. When she was alone, she'd take out the quilt, fondle it and drape it around her shoulders. She'd breathe in the caring that the gift represented and be less afraid.

Each day Calley walked the three miles down Pine Mountain to visit the site of her new home. Approaching the clearing, Peter heard her singing. Concealed behind the hazelnut bushes, he observed her joy. She was dancing in and out through the studdings and whirling in the middle of the would-be rooms, singing over and over again, "It's mine for love—it's mine for love." Peter withdrew into the shadows of the pines, not knowing quite how to share. He simply let his heart dance with her.

The neighborhood crew wrapped the inner surface of the studs with a heavy layer of tarpaper. They carried slabs from Bill Parson's mill ("a wedding present, Peter," Bill had said) and nailed them carefully on the outer walls. Peter's extra work in the woods on weekends meant that he could buy windows and hardware for the doors. Someday, maybe they could even have wallboard on the inside dividers, but tarpaper would have to do for now. Calley said that'd be all right. She'd put up some pictures cut from magazines to make it cheerful.

Peter worked every spare minute on into the fall. He shaped a table and four chairs ("just in case we have company"). A rough double-platform bed was nailed into a corner of the tiny bedroom along with some shelves for their things (" 'til I can get a chest made"). Calley sewed together burlap bags for a mattress and stuffed it with straw. She added a touch of cedar twigs "to make it smell good."

Calley was sewing the last seam late one afternoon alone in the cabin when she sensed someone in the next room. She heard a humming sound and saw a shadow fall across the doorway. In a moment it framed the grey-wrapped figure of Gletha.

"Hello, Gletha. You scared me some. I didn't know anybody was around. I ain't seen you since you brought Mary's quilt up the mountain. I'm keeping it as a surprise for Peter on our wedding night. It'll keep us real warm atop this mattress."

"I brung you something for your mattress."

"Why that's real sweet of you, Gletha. What did you bring?"

Gletha held out a young mullein leaf that had survived the early frost. Calley took it and stroked its green velvet surface.

"It's like touching a baby's cheek," she said. "But why should I put it in our mattress?"

"It'll help keep you safe—and pertect any babies that come along from the whooping cough."

"Oh, Gletha, I'd never a'known that. I'll slip it right in before I sew up this corner."

As she turned to insert the gift, she said, "Sit a while and talk. I can't offer you nothin'. Florrie's givin' us her old cookstove from their back shed, but we ain't moved it yet, so I can't even offer you some coffee."

She turned back, only to discover that the stately, grey-clad woman had disappeared. Looking out the window, she saw Gletha passing close to a grazing doe at the clearing's edge. The doe didn't even look up as the late afternoon shadows closed over Gletha. Calley slipped a finger through the mattress slit and stroked the soft leaf one last time before finishing her task.

For the bride-to-be, the two most important parts of the wedding preparation were the special dress and the "rose o' love." From girlhood Calley had dreamed of a rose o' love to wear at her throat on her wedding day.

As a child living with Jennie Mauldin (who was Aunt Jennie to everyone in the neighborhood), she had watched her make roses o' love for every girl married in the township. She was famous for making beautiful silk flowers, their edges hemmed with the tiniest stitches anyone had ever seen.

Aunt Jennie had told her tales of coming to the north country by ox-cart, bringing with her from Pennsylvania three treasures that her husband Warren thought extravagant: a little parlor pump organ, a cast iron mold to make the Easter lamb cake and her oak "treasure chest" filled with fabrics and lace, little china dolls and old letters. Calley remembered a beautiful piece of pale pink silk.

The day after Peter asked her to marry him, she had walked along the rutted road toward Aunt Jennie's house. Soon after her arrival she worked up her courage to ask the elderly woman a special favor: "Aunt Jennie, I know your hands are awful crippled and holdin' a needle is terrible hard, but you once said that if I was good you might make me a rose 'o love to wear on my weddin' day. Well, Peter Stopes has finally asked me. Do you think it might be possible to still make one more rose—just for me?"

Aunt Jennie hugged her close for a moment. "I just don't know, Calley. These old fingers are terrible stiff. Gletha's had the boys cut the oil glands out of their trapline mink. She does something to 'em—and I rub the concoction on my hands.

We'll just have to wait and see."

Calley dreamed of the rose. She just waited and hoped. The dress was simpler. There was no money for a store-bought, ready-made one—or even for store-bought fabric. But the elevator in town carried chickenfeed and flour in patterned cotton bags. If you could find four sacks that matched, you'd sew yourself a real fine cotton dress. When the bags first started arriving, women demanded that the workers in the elevator move great piles of feed to find the proper combinations of paisleys, flowers and geometrical designs. Then the owner's son, Gary Porter, put up a badly lettered sign whose intent was clear: ALL FEED SOLD FROM THE TOP OF THE PILE ONLEE AND NO EXCEPSHUNS! From then on you'd hear women describing various patterns as they talked on the party telephone line. Everyone secretly listening in would jot down what was available. There was much swapping.

Peter and Calley drove to town in his old Chevy pickup, supposedly to get feed for his parents' chickens—but really to find sacks for a wedding dress.

The August sun beat down on the metal skin of the elevator. The feed room was like a furnace. The heavy odor of the grain seemed to coat the inside of one's lungs. Calley looked critically at the hundreds of sacks. Nothing seemed quite fine enough for her special day.

Peter said, "Let's get out o' here, Calley. You're gonna' pass out from the heat."

Just as she turned to go, she saw them: two sacks close to the top—and two buried about fifty-three sacks down near the bottom of the pile. They were perfect—tiny, delicate pink roses on a field of white.

"Well now, Gary," she said, "we'll just take them four." She pointed to the chosen bags.

Gary exploded, his nerves frayed by the intense heat. "Calley, we was together in Aunt Theo's school, so I know you kin read. Didn't you see that sign? I don't move no extra feed—and I don't save sacks for nobody! You kin have the two near the top and take yer chances on the others!"

Calley burst into tears. "I only intend to be married once. Can't you do it for me just this one time?"

Peter stepped forward. "Gary, I'll move the grain. You won't have to touch a single bag."

"I can't let you do that. You'll keel over in this heat, and then it'll be my fault."

Unheeding, Peter was already moving the mountain of feed.

An hour later, the two were driving home—with the four bags printed with tiny roses. Calley had insisted that one bag be put inside the cab on the seat between them so she could touch it and dream. A sweat-drenched Peter dreamed along with her.

The December wedding day dawned bright and clear with an unusual melting edge. Calley was up before the sun. She pulled the quilt out of its hiding place and sat wrapped in it for a long time. She wanted to feel all the love and courage she could as she faced everybody on this special day.

She fixed breakfast for herself and her father. Emil came in from the barn with a pail of milk. His eyes glistened with tears and laughter as he remembered his own wedding day nearly seventeen years before.

Calley poured the milk into the great stone crocks so the cream would rise. They sat down at the table.

Emil looked at her. She smiled back at him, not even worrying about her twisted teeth. He said, "Calley, I don't know what's come over you lately. The frightened forest shadow which was once my daughter is a smiling young woman."

Calley responded, "Pa, I gotta' show you somethin' special."

She disappeared into her bedroom and returned in a moment with the Dresden Plate quilt. She explained, "I think this is what done it, Pa. Gletha brought me this quilt from Mary since I didn't have none of my own. She called it a 'loan of love.' Every time I put it around me, it's like I'm being hugged by everybody what put a needle to it. I realize I don't have to be scared no more."

She twirled the quilt around her shoulders like an ermine robe. Emil laughed, leaped to his feet and caught her in a bear hug—quilt and all. He held her for a long time. She felt his tears on her forehead. He said quietly, "My premature baby's grown from her peach crate into a queen."

Releasing her, he continued, "I'll catch the dishes. You get yerself ready to go down the mountain."

She wrapped the quilt in well-bleached towels and tied it

into a bundle with binder twine. Emil stepped into her room to pick up the final bundle of her belongings. Calley carried the quilt. Her wedding dress was already awaiting her in the cloakroom of Bear Run School.

As they passed Elvira's grave, they paused. Calley rested the quilt on the ill-carved headstone and whispered, "It's okay, Ma, there's been folks around to raise me. There's plenty of love to be both given and loaned."

They continued down the mountain.

All the township folk gathered in Bear Run School, which doubled as church for the occasional Bible student who drove out from Spruce Crossing to "practice preach." Pastor Pelius McDowell from the Lakeside Church of Jesus Risen came out from town special to do the ceremony.

In the cloakroom, now off-limits to everyone but the bride, Calley put on the dress, lovingly made from the hard-won sacks. It seemed as if half the women in the neighborhood appeared to "put in the finishing touches." Even Florrie was there to add a stitch to her waist—and thereby more clearly confirm whether or not the bride-to-be was "in the family way." She was disappointed to discover the same fragile waist she'd always envied in this girl in contrast to her own plump daughters.

Looking at herself in the cracked mirror with the flawed silvering which hung over the washstand at the end of the cloakroom, Calley decided the dress was beautiful. There was only one thing missing: the rose o' love. Aunt Jennie had not said a thing since Calley asked months ago. Jennie got more frail with each passing week, and folks kept saying how terrible her arthritis was.

Fiddler Jake played lively melodies as the guests arrived at Bear Run School. There were surprised comments as people noticed the "altar"—usually a bare schoolroom table with Todd Tolliver's hand-carved wooden cross on it. Today it shown resplendently, covered by the Dresden Plate quilt.

Calley waited in the cloakroom so that neither Peter nor anyone else could see her. The door opened. It was not her father ready to walk her to the front. It was Aunt Jennie, moving painfully toward her—a small tissue-papered parcel in her twisted hands.

Calley unwrapped it. In the cloakroom's dim light the silk rose seemed to glow from a kind of inner power. It was as if the December sun had melted the snow from Jennie's garden and discovered there a perfect rose preserved from summer. Aunt Jennie grimaced with pain as she pushed a pin through the stiff stem and fastened the flower at the "V" of Calley's dress.

"Calley, I've always loved you special. It was love that kept the needle firm in the fabric. Let it always remind you that love is sometimes painful—but that beauty can grow out of pain." Jennie held Calley close for a moment. Then she slowly hobbled out to join the guests.

Fiddler Jake began the "Wedding March." Calley's dad took her arm, and they began their walk together. Standing away from the rest of the guests in a corner of the schoolroom was Gletha, the goatlady. As Calley passed by, Gletha stretched out a hand and sprinkled rosemary leaves in the petals of the rose o' love and whispered, "That's so love will last."

When the ceremony was over, folk crowded round to wish the couple luck—and to admire in awestruck tones the glowing beauty of the rose o' love—and to run their fingers over the delicate stitchery on the altar table.

After the sharing of refreshments which everybody had brought and a bit of dancing, folk began to drift home before the early fall of December darkness. Peter assured Aunt Theo that he'd close up the school building proper. He wanted to spend a few moments alone with Calley in this place of their joy.

Calley took Peter's hand and led him to the table. She told him the story of the quilt. He lifted the cross to its place on the back shelf. She folded the quilt.

After closing up the school, Calley draped the quilt over the shoulders of their sheepskin coats. They walked to their new home in the early evening starlight.

That night they lay in each other's arms beneath the "loan of love" and expressed that other dimension: love freely given.

The day after the wedding, Peter came into the cabin holding something behind his back. He was grinning broadly. "I just came from Bear Run Store. I got you somethin' special."

"Oh, Peter! We ain't got no money for anything special."

"It didn't cost nothin'. Aunt Minnie T. says you can count it as a wedding present."

He held out to her an oblong glass box. "Aunt Minnie T. says this once held bracelets—but she's not carryin' 'em any longer. Yer rose o' love should just fit in here."

Calley rushed to the bedroom and took the rose from its place of honor on the shelf. It did indeed fit in its special case. Calley put the case in the center of the table. Peter took her in his arms, and they watched the winter light sparkle on the glass as the sun set on that late-Advent day.

"Calley, we got our own Bethlehem Star right here in our cabin."

As the seasons changed, Calley changed. Word spread that Calley and Peter would have a child born close to their first anniversary.

It was shortly before Christmas when most folk saw it—or heard about it as word spread by way of the party line. The sky glowed an angry red—a sure sign that a forest cabin was going up in flames. Folk rushed toward the source, knowing it had to be Calley and Peter's tarpapered home.

A circle of neighbors stood helplessly around the burning cabin. The old cookstove had exploded. The couple escaped without severe burns. Everything they owned was destroyed—except the Dresden Plate quilt. They stood wrapped in the "loan of love," amazed that they'd escaped with both the quilt and their lives. The protecting fabric was supplemented by person after person coming to them and weaving together a great community embrace. There was no longer any thought in their minds that they had to be beholden to anybody.

They all walked across the field together to Peter's parents' house—a silent community of comfort.

As Calley lay in Peter's embrace, crowded into his childhood bed, her last words were, "Peter, the only thing we can't replace is the rose o' love."

"But, Calley, our love's special. We got a kind of love that we never need to replace."

"I'll still miss it glowing there like the Bethlehem Star."

"But," he countered, "we still got the quilt. We know that

even when the road is rocky, we got the touching hands of folks to bear us up."

They started in the middle of the night—the birth contractions. By morning an exhausted Calley lay in the dawn light, a new daughter on the pillow beside her. Peter dozed in a bedside chair.

Nobody heard her enter. But Gletha, the goatlady, appeared in the doorway of the room. Peter awoke with a start. In his confusion, he jumped up to order her away. Then he saw it. In her extended hands was the undamaged glass case. Within it glowed the rose o' love.

"Gletha! Where did you find it? How could it survive when even the windows melted in the heat?"

She replied, "Mullein and rosemary keep all they touch free." Then she disappeared.

Peter put the resurrected Star of Bethlehem on the pillow by his sleeping daughter. When Calley awoke and turned her head to look at the baby, she saw that the rose o' love had doubled.

Peter stood up and put the encased rose on a shelf above the bed. He removed his boots and overalls and climbed under the special quilt. He put his tiny daughter in the crook of one arm and reached for Calley's hand with the other.

He said softly, "I'm glad we're calling her Elvira. It's such a beautiful name. It really should continue beyond the grave. Beyond the grave—I s'pose I shouldn't be thinking sad kinds of thoughts right now. But we were almost killed in the fire. We thought the rose o' love was lost. We managed to save the quilt to shelter us. It makes me think: everything in this world, even our very lives, is on loan. We shouldn't waste a minute on anything but love. I love you, Calley."

She placed the fingers of his free hand to her lips. "I love you, Peter."

Elvira stirred. Peter snuggled her against his cheek. They slept deeply.

Lanterns in the Snow

My father feared the darkness. His fear deepened in the gloom of December as Christmas, the time of light, drew near. As long as the kerosene lamps were ablaze from sundown until bedtime, he could endure the star-shot blackness that surrounded our tiny shack.

In the Yuletide season, his spirits healed a bit as he watched the lamplight reflected on the Christmas tree decorations: the single ten-cent package of tinsel—bought years before and carefully removed from each ensuing tree because there was no money to buy new—and the patches of sparkle on the eleven peeling red balls which had graced evergreens the twenty years of my parents' life together.

When my father was at the height of his anger or the depths of withdrawal, Gletha would appear, a pail of warm goat's milk in her hand, its secret additives disguised by a dash of Karo Syrup. He would swear and order her out of the house and forbid my ever moving through the woods with her again. However, her offerings occasionally shortened his times of darkness. To this day, I wish I knew the healing herbal combination in her gifts.

The Advent season when I was nine glows in my memory. Thirty-seven inches of snow had fallen in three weeks. Four days before Christmas, the wind-driven flakes began to fall again. My father and I fought our way to the barns to care for the cows, sheep and horses. During a break in the storm, we watched a tragic wilderness ballet: a deer floundering in the deep drifts killed and devoured by a pack of wolves.

There was little to do during those blizzard-shrouded days. However, one pastime went on incessantly: rubbernecking. There were eighteen families on the party telephone line— each with its own distinguishable "ring." Our ring was effected by someone cranking out a short and a long and a short and a long. When another family's ring was heard, everyone on the party line became adept at covering the mouthpiece with one hand while quietly easing the receiver off the hook with the other in order to listen in on the conversation.

My Aunt Floy was among the more persistent rubberneckers. She had one handicap: a small dog named Yip who tore loose with a horrendous cascade of barking at the slightest provocation. As Floy listened, she'd forget to cover the mouthpiece. Yip would sight an offending squirrel through the window and let out a torrent of noise. One of the callers might well shout, "Floy, git off the phone. We want to talk about you."

The blizzard continued through Christmas Eve Day. Each passing hour brought more concern to Mother and me. We had used the last of the kerosene—and God only knew when we'd be able to get to town to purchase more. The candles, too, were gone. We faced the prospect of celebrating the Christ Child's birth in fear-filled darkness fought by my father with outbursts of physically expressed anger.

As night erased the pines on the far edge of the clearing, my father and I came in from the barns. He had clung to my hand like a jittery child as we made our way through the thick-falling snow. Entering the tiny kitchen, he opened the lid to the cast iron cookstove. The red glow from the coals reflected on the tears coursing down his face as he cried out to my mother, "Mary, can't you do something about the dark?"

My mother moved to the wall-mounted phone and cranked out three shorts and a long. The booming voice of a mile-distant neighbor could be heard rolling out over the receiver. My mother pleaded with him: "Ted, can you spare a little kerosene for tonight? We got terrible sickness over here. Frank is really down. We just can't face spending a night with no light."

"Mary, I got a little extree, but it's still snowin' to beat the devil, and there ain't no way I can get it to you unless the snow stops. There's not much chance of that happenin'."

"Well, bye, Ted—and thanks anyhow. Don't let yerself git blowed away. And listen—you all have a Merry Christmas."

She hung up the receiver and paused for a moment, leaning wearily against the wall beneath the phone. Daddy had seated himself in his creaking rocking chair by the potbellied stove, clenching and unclenching his fists.

I stood by the window, staring at the last ghosts of blizzard-shattered light. Then I saw her: Gletha, the goatlady. With her soft grey cloths flowing behind her, she appeared to be riding the drifting snow, waving her arms in a slow cadence as if conducting a symphony of the elements. The wind gentled. The falling snow lessened. Through the clouds, burst the incredibly bright light of a full moon starkly detailing every aspect of the Christmas Eve landscape. I blinked my eyes in disbelief—and Gletha was gone.

Then they appeared like fireflies in the distance—some from the north and some from the south: lanterns—seventeen lanterns growing larger as their bearers came nearer. My father heard my gasp of amazement. He stumbled to the window and shoved me roughly aside. He cried out, "Mary—my God—the lights—look at the lights!"

They came on that Christmas Eve, the light bearers. But they bore more than light. Though jobs were scarce and gardens had dried up and the snow was too deep to care for traplines, everybody brought something to share. Tillie Mauldin had come up with the makings of mincemeat pie. Bill Cooley had some ground venison. Gyp Matthews brought corn to pop. Thirty people or more crowded into the tiny living room and kitchen. In their midst was Gletha, the goatlady, with her magic pail of milk and secret powders and the dash of Karo Syrup. For those few moments on that magic evening, the fact that she was suspected of witchcraft—and smelled pungently of the goats she cared for—was forgotten.

She suddenly lifted her hands, and silence settled on the celebration. She said quietly, "I think there's good spirits a'bornin' here." She raised her rich voice in "Silent Night," and everyone joined in. The Child in the manger became as close as the snowbound sheepsheds fifty paces off.

We sang and laughed and shared far into the night. Ted rolled in our kerosene barrel, and everyone poured half a lantern-full into it. We would not be without light.

As the crowd moved out to the front yard shouting Christmas greetings, Gletha's voice was joined by all in one last hymn, "Amazing Grace." As folk, lanterns in hand, moved out across the moonlit snow, blessed on their way by the sung words of God's gifting, their pattern assumed the shape of a gigantic moving star. I knew that our Bethlehem had been visited by flesh-shaped hope.

The Ladyslipper

"It was the left socket!" I insisted.

"It wasn't!" protested Gletha. "It was the right. Don't go a'contradictin' them as is older'n you."

Having stopped Gletha's story in mid-stream, I settled into the arrowback chair ever assigned to me and resigned myself to the fact that I had lost the argument. Having previously been consoled with a cracked mug of warm goat's milk sweetened with Karo, I stared through the grimy pane of glass across the snow-covered field where the wind had already obliterated the tracks of my boots. My nine-year-old legs were still damp to the crotch from my struggles storyward through the tail end of a late-spring blizzard.

Gletha adjusted her grey draperies. She was every inch an oracle in the battered, over-stuffed chair. She drifted back to the tale again after my impertinent interruption. I rode into my own memory on the drone of her voice. This was a story I'd lived as well. Her words cued the graveside pictures to which I added the color of my own creation.

It had happened the previous spring. The anemones and wild strawberries were budding. The ground would soon be sufficiently thawed so that I could set out my pocketgopher traps. I was, as usual, alone in the forest, savoring and hating my solitude. The trees were aching to leaf out, but the reluctant buds seemed to hesitate before the possibility of a final storm.

I had followed a track which I'd never seen before. It wound deeper and deeper into the heavier timber on the distant slope. I had to know where it led. The more I concentrated on the faint marking on the woodland floor, the less I was aware of the solitariness of my search.

So intent was I on the obscure track that I almost stumbled over it: the wolf-torn carcass of the deer.

It had been a bad winter for wolves. The snow had been deep. Prey was scarce. The grey shadows had circled our sheepfold and were kept at a distance only by my father's rifle. With the first wolf howl, he went for his gun. My mother would cry silently out of fear, not of the wolves, but of what the man, whose mental illness deepened during the short, dark days, might do to himself or to us as he carried death in his hands.

I stared at the bits of pelt and the blood still fresh on the ground. I realized that I must have scared them off on my approach. I shivered with the realization that I was probably being watched from the sunless forest depths. I desperately hoped the scavengers had had their fill. The old hunters sitting around the potbellied stove in Bear Run Store filled our young heads with gory tales of mangled children.

Trapper Art's rendition had been particularly memorable, colored by the fact that two pairs of ears listened from the vantage point of the candy counter. My best friend, Charlie, and I, ever penniless, squatted by the glass case, hoping Aunt Minnie T. might pass by and offer us a handful of horehound drops. We were distracted from hope by the stark terror inherent in the ensuing narration:

"Now, you gotta' be r-e-a-l careful-like whenever you go out into the woods. Don't never go alone, 'cause before you know it you'll look off into the underbrush to yer left and you'll see four grey shadows movin' along at an e-a-s-y pace right with you. Whatever you do, don't run. That'll just excite 'em to attack. You might wanta' just walk a wee tad faster to get where you're goin'. The real problem begins to develop when you look up and notice that a couple of 'em have broke off from the foursome and crossed over behind you. With two on your left and two on your right you'd better walk even a wee tad faster, 'cause you'd better be arrivin' at where you want to get in a v-e-r-y short period of time. If you look up again and notice that two's broke off from your left and your right and you now got one before you and one behind you and one on either side, you'd just better sit down where you are and say your prayers, 'cause that's attack formation. Sure as shootin' they'll turn, and before you can say 'Jack Robinson,' they'll tear you limb from limb. Once folk miss you and start the search, the only thing they'll find is the buckles from your bib overalls layin' in the forest path."

By this time, Charlie and I were cowering in each other's arms. The only antidote had been Gletha, the goatlady, who insisted that wolves were gentle, caring creatures. She always called them her babies.

Her surmise was dismissed by Trapper Art with a flip comment, "What would the witchlady know about such things?" The men would grin sagely at one another.

I deliberated for a moment. I was miles from home. Should I retrace my steps or follow the promptings of my curiosity? My memory of Gletha's evaluation of the nature of the predators overcame me. I went on.

I was soon aware of shadows that at first glance belonged securely to lightning-blasted cedars. Then their grey outlines shifted slightly in my direction. I began to move more quickly. I could now distinguish four great beasts loping equidistant from me. The terrible realization dawned on me. The old hunters had been right. I was being stalked. I remembered the bits of deer hair and the blood on the ground. All that searchers would discover would be stains on the ancient path—and the buckles of my faded bib overalls.

Remembering Trapper Art's instructions, I increased my pace slightly. So did they. Without really seeing the transformation in pattern, I was aware that there were now two on my right and two on my left. They were inexorably moving toward attack. I picked up my pace again, having no idea whether or not I was heading in the direction of safety.

Hoping against hope that the wolves might decide they were full from their meal of deer meat and so would retire to their lair deep in the forest, I kept steadfastly to the faint trail. It seemed to be heading up toward Fever Pond. If I could just get to the burned-out shack that had been lived in by the family who died of scarlet fever, I might find a place of refuge. Even better, I might get as far as the shack of Old Otto which had remained untenanted since Mayetta and Todd Tolliver had gotten back together.

My hopes were shattered when I became aware that the pattern had changed a final time. A single beast flanked me on either side—and I was being both followed and led. The moment of their turning on me could not be far off.

With a cry of terror, I ran deeper into the woods, still keeping to the old ruts. Suddenly I was in an overgrown clearing. The remnants of the charred house stood at the far side. I headed for it as quickly as possible. I knew it had a root cellar in which a pursued boy might hope for sanctuary.

My foot caught on a hard object, and I was thrown headlong to the ground. The upper part of my body seemed to have fallen into some kind of hole. I lay slightly stunned, waiting for the inevitable: my total dismemberment by savage teeth.

Time was suspended. I don't know how long I laid, torso downward, eyes tightly closed.

Her voice cut through my fear: "Boy, what are you doin' down in that hole?"

I glanced quickly over my shoulder. There she was, Gletha, the goatlady. The soft cloths were streaming out behind her in the spring wind, making it look for all the world like she'd just alighted. She was flanked by the great beasts sitting docilely on their haunches like dogs panting from the exertion of their pursuit.

"G-G-Gletha, fly! They're f-foolin' you. They're really planning to take you apart!"

"Rogee, don't be a dumb ox. Get yerself out of that hole!" Even in my extremity, something in me prepared to do battle with her over the use of that hated name: "Gletha, how many times do I gotta' tell you...."

As I spoke, I shifted my position so that I might squiggle my way feet-first out of the hole. My words were choked out by an involuntary scream. I discovered myself eyeball-to-empty-eye-socket with a small white skull at the bottom of the hole.

"Gletha, run for it! There's a skull down here—all that's left of a kid they've attacked before. Trapper Art was right."

I felt something hard under my left shoulder. I knew it had

to be the buckles from the victim's bib overalls.

"Boy, get yerself outta' there."

I shuddered my way up and out, avoiding the wolves who now seemed to be watching me in a friendly fashion as if they wanted to be petted.

My argumentative reply was cut short by my glance falling on the small skull at the bottom of the hole. From this vantage point I noticed what I had not seen before: the ladyslipper growing through the right socket—its golden flower dancing a spring ballet choreographed by the breeze.

"Look," I said, pointing authoritatively at the white remainder. "The wolves have done in one kid already!"

"That wasn't my babies. That were the scarlet fever. See what you fell over."

It was then that I saw the heavy, rough board beginning to decay which had fallen at an angle to conveniently trip me. The words burned on the board were faded but clear: CELESTE b. Oct. 3, 1917 d. March 21, 1918.

"That's the grave of one of the Schocken kids. Whole family died up here. Yer Uncle Pud was a'cuttin' wood over there and discovered the last one—Timmy. He was twelve. He was sick. Pud found him dead halfway out of the burned-out house. He buried him in that grove of birch. Celeste though—she was the prettiest little thing. I loved to touch her."

Gletha took my arm and led me back to the grave's edge. She knelt and reached for the ladyslipper. She didn't pick it. She simply stroked it with the tip of her rough index finger. "Feels like a baby's cheek"—and she guided my thumb to follow her pattern.

"Folks somehow really do live forever. Somehow. Somehow. Remember, Rogee. If you can be in touch with what you fear most, you'll prob'ly discover inside it something that's healing and beautiful."

Still kneeling on the grave edge, she transferred our attention to the nearest wolf. She stroked my thumb across the soft fur of its throat, still blood-flecked from the deer. The great beast grinned its appreciation. Then she returned my hand to the ladyslipper.

As my finger followed the dancing flower, I believed in eternal life with more conviction than I ever did when the shouting evangelists pled for goodness and promised the reward of the pearly gates.

She continued to croon, "Feels like a baby's cheek." I rode the wave of her song back to the snowbound present.

"Gletha, I still say it was the left socket. Gletha, will I really live forever?"

"Somehow. Somehow."

The Mother's Day Gift

"Gletha, how come you and Pud never had no babies?"

She gave me one of those none-of-your-beeswax looks and responded, "I got you, and that's more'n enough!"

"Aw, Gletha. You're not my mother. I got one of those already, and that's more'n enough! You both couldn't have made me."

"Makin' has nothin' to do with birthin'. Every time you're with me, I make you just a little bit. You got two mothers or more whether you like it or not."

It was the Saturday before Mother's Day. The previous day had been a nightmare. Each kid in third grade was to make a present and card for his or her mother. I could never make a crayon do what the teacher thought it should do—and I always had rather definite ideas about what I wanted to create.

I had a terrible battle with Miss Strasser (who had been my teacher at the school in Spruce Crossing since the old Bear Run schoolhouse was closed). I wanted to put a beautiful yellow dandelion on the front cover of the card with "I love you, Mom" painfully scrawled in pink on the inside. Miss Strasser felt that dandelions weren't good enough for mothers—I had to draw roses. I'd seen few roses, but I'd seen lots of dandelions. She insisted that I do what she said. I tried to compromise on a handsome purple thistle. She got really mad and said I'd better spend half an hour in the cloakroom thinking about co-operation. All I thought about was how much I hated Miss Strasser. So much for the morning!

In the afternoon we were given small pictures of a family of rabbits. We were to color them carefully, glue them on blocks of wood and shellac them. Our mothers would have lovely plaques to hang on their dining room walls. The rabbits, we were firmly instructed, were to be colored brown. While Miss Strasser was at her desk correcting spelling tests, I determinedly, but carefully, colored my rabbits bright red so that they would match the rhino I had created the year before. She passed through the classroom a bit later, admiring the uniformly brown bunnies of the other children. I felt her gaze on my back. I hunkered down over my beautiful creation, hoping she'd pass on by—or the principal would call her to the office—or there'd be a sudden forest fire. She grabbed me by the shoulder and pulled me upright, asking me, in the process, how many times she had told me to sit up straight and not ruin my posture.

She saw my scarlet rabbits. The ever-present ruler in her hand cracked down sharply on my recalcitrant knuckles. She snatched the paper from my desk and held it up for all to see. Snickers enveloped the classroom. I spent the rest of the afternoon in the cloakroom "thinking about co-operation"— and how much I hated Miss Strasser.

When I climbed wearily from the bus and paused at my place of refuge, Gletha slammed a tin cup of warm goat's milk sweetened with Karo Syrup on the worn oilcloth table cover. "You look awful. Got somethin' weighin' on your mind?"

"I ain't got no present for Mom for Mother's Day. Miss Strasser threw away my dandelions and my red rabbits."

Gletha stared out through the small, dirt-streaked window. "I wanted to be a teacher once. I don't think I'd a'throwed away anybody's dandelions and rabbits."

A tear coursed down her cheek. I reached across the table and patted her thin elbow. "I wish you was my teacher, Gletha."

She looked at me, pushed a strand of hair off her forehead and said, "What do you think I spend mosta' my time doin'?"

I finished the milk and stepped to the door. The May sunlight was making the last vestiges of the late-April blizzard disappear.

"Gletha, let's go hikin' in the woods. No tellin' what we

might find on a day like this."

"Shouldn't we be makin' somethin' for your mom?"

"Naw, we got plenty o' time later. Maybe I'll find somethin' in the woods that'll be just perfect."

"Sure—like a pot o' gold at the end of a rainbow."

I looked at her quickly. With Gletha you could never tell if she was serious or not, but the quirky smile playing about her lips showed me that I was being teased again.

She closed the shack door. "All right, Rogee, let's see what's happenin' over beyond Old Lady Slough."

Anger flooded over me and tears sprang to my eyes. I shouted at her for the umpteenth time, "D-D-Dammit all, Gletha. You know I hate that n-name. Don't you ever call me Rogee again or I'll run away and never speak to you and then you'll be alone here with your dumb goats and Pud snorin' away in the shack."

"Young man, you just stop your cussin'. The best Mother's Day present you could give to yer mom would be to stop cussin'."

"I don't have to stop cussin' for you. My dad's the best cusser in Bear Run Township an' he laughs and says I'm beginnin' to sound like a growed-up man. That's the only good thing he ever says to me."

Gletha looked at me for a long moment. "Kid, I'll continue to call you Rogee 'cause maybe if you hear it enough from somebody who loves you it won't be so bad when you hear it from somebody who's tryin' to hurt you. As for your dad, pay him no mind. I swear, he's sick in the head to talk to a boy like that."

She reached out and took my hand, and we headed east toward Old Lady Slough. The late-spring breeze was at our backs. The filmy pieces of cloth she wrapped herself in began to billow out ahead of us, seeming to draw us through the scrub pine with increasing speed. She began to hum one of her strange tunes. The hair on the back of my neck cater-pillared up as I felt myself seeming to float just above the pine-needle-covered earth through the warm May light.

Suddenly, Gletha gasped, and we came to an abrupt halt. I heard something moving on the forest floor—and then a des-perate, high-pitched whine. Four timber wolves were circled around something struggling and crying out in the under-brush at the foot of a rotting, lightning-blasted tree. They were motionless—like statues carved out of hillside granite.

"Gletha, wolves!" I whispered. "Let's get outta' here!"

She shushed me with a look. We crept closer. The wolves paid no attention to us. They were mesmerized by the struggle playing itself out in front of them. A month-old wolf cub, early-born, was caught in a sharp-toothed trap. The razor-edged teeth had nearly torn off the left front leg at the shoulder.

Gletha gave a low moan and glided quickly toward the injured animal. She still had a tight grip on my hand so I followed, wishing to be as quiet as she but stumbling over every root my feet encountered. I kept wishing we'd continued to float.

Gletha took the trap in her delicate but amazingly strong hands and carefully sprung it open, releasing the injured beast. Continuing to whimper, it moved its head to watch Gletha through pain-glazed eyes.

Gletha unwound one of her pieces of cloth. She slipped the cloth ever-so-gently under the torn limb. She arranged two sticks on either side of the bleeding leg. She took handfuls of moist moss from the base of a shattered tree and packed it around the leg between the sticks. Then she tightly bound it all together. She gently picked up the suffering animal and rocked it in her arms.

I'd been so intent on watching her doctor the fragile cub that I had not seen one of the grey statues move. There, at Gletha's side as she knelt on the forest floor cradling the tiny wild thing and singing her strange song, was a full-uddered female wolf. I held my breath, certain that the wolf would tear at the circling arms to free her baby from its final entrapment. But the wolf stood there. Then she nuzzled her baby nestled in its strange cradle, turned and disappeared into the forest.

"Gletha," I whispered, "I thought we were gonners."

"Rogee, you don't listen so good. Ain't I told you a hundred times before that the wolves are all my babies?"

"Gletha, that's dumb. You told me back at the shack that I was sorta' your kid. Now you say the wolves are your babies too. That makes me brother to the wolves!"

She stared at me for a moment. "Well, you could do worse."

We moved on the May breeze back to the shack. It was late afternoon. The goats were gathering for milking. Old Gert, the best milker, had already mounted the pine stump for Gletha's strong hands to strip out the milk. The three legged cat was in its usual place, ready for supper.

The maaing of the goats was stilled as we approached. They smelled an enemy—but seemed unthreatened. Gletha knelt at the pine stump and placed the cub's mouth at Old Gert's overflowing teat. The tiny beast began to suck, and Gletha smiled as she knelt.

Gletha handed the now-sleeping cub to me while she finished the milking.

"Gletha, what are we goin' to do now with this unexpected baby?"

The early evening chill had settled in. The little beast in my arms was quivering. "It really needs to be by that big, old potbellied stove in your livin' room that your daddy keeps so redded up all night just in case we get a May chill."

Without another word I set off through the cut-over timber and across the clearing toward our house. The kerosene lamp was already lighted on the kitchen table. As I neared the house, I shouted, "Mom! Dad! Come quick! See what I've got!"

My mother appeared at the door. "Hush yer yellin'! Yer dad's terrible depressed again. He's sittin' by the stove in the living room with his head in his hands. Now you just hush."

Then she saw the small torn creature in my arms. Its fur and my shirtfront were flecked with blood.

"Oh, the poor thing! What in the world will we do with it?"

Without a word I walked away from her into the living room. My father sat in the rocking chair, lighted only from the glow of the fire through the isinglass window on the stovefront. His face was a changing mask of tears and terror as images none of us could comprehend tore at him inside.

"Dad," I said quietly.

He lifted his head quickly, startled into immediate anger.

I stepped closer to him. "Look, Dad."

He saw the wounded cub. His face softened. He reached out his arms and took the sleeping animal in his lap.

I headed to the kitchen to wash up for a supper of cold chicken and bread pudding.

My mother and I paused in the living room on our way to bed. The wolf and the man were both asleep in the fireglow.

The next morning I awakened and headed for the rocking chair. Dad was nowhere to be seen. He had lined a box with a piece of my mother's new quilt batting which she'd been saving for her "Star of Texas" quilt. The box was carefully placed where the stove's warmth would be caught. The cub was still curled in contented sleep.

A step was heard outside. My dad came grinning into the kitchen, a pail of foaming milk in his hand.

"Hey, kid, that's a beautiful new friend you brought home last night. I think he's gonna' make it. Now, run this milk through the separator while I feed the sheep."

My mother watched my dad whistle his way to the sheep-shed through the cool glow of a May morning, no longer on the violent edge of his private darkness.

"Hey, Mom, I'm really sorry. Here it is Mother's Day, and I ain't got a card or a present or nothin'. Old Miss Strasser spoiled everything for me."

She put an arm around my shoulders. "You gave me the best present possible—your dad's grin."

The next day being Monday, I boarded the school bus for another day with Miss Strasser. Second period, right after recess, was always recitation time. I hated those moments more than any other hour of the day. It was agony for me to get more than a few sentences out due to my terrible stammer. Miss Strasser was sure I wouldn't stammer if I really tried to concentrate and think about each word and speak very, very slowly. I should pretend to be a little train engine moving with slow determination up a mountain. She told me that in front of the whole class. From that day on, whenever I stood up to try to speak, and she wasn't looking, the boys in the class would circle their elbows at their sides like train wheels and pull imaginary bell cords. How I wished the country school had not been consolidated into town. I dreamed of being back in Bear Run School with Aunt Theo.

On the way into Spruce Crossing, I shared my weekend adventures with my friend Charlie. We always ate half a sandwich on the way in. He wanted to trade. I didn't blame him. My sandwiches were spread with fresh-churned butter and blueberry jam on homemade bread. His were lard and cinnamon on day-old store-bought bread. I went ahead and traded since he was my only friend—and he never teased me about my stammer.

Charlie's eyes grew large as I related the events of my weekend with the wolf cub. "Gee, Rog. You got somethin' great for recitation time. I bet since it's so good you won't have no trouble at all stammerin'. Everybody will be so into the story that they'll forget all about teasin' you."

Bolstered by Charlie's confidence, I really did look forward to recitation time. When Miss Strasser called for volunteers to lead off the sharing, my hand shot up.

"Why, Roger! Do you really want to go first? What a lovely surprise. Now remember, boys and girls, today we are to share a true story about something that happened over the weekend."

As I walked to the front of the classroom, I saw the elbows of the boys move into "little engine" positions. I took a deep breath—and a long look at Charlie, whose eyes were closed and whose lips were moving as if he were praying for me.

I swung into the narration. There was shocked silence at the clarity of my speech. One by one the elbows dropped as the entire class fell under the spell of my tale of the wild. The only movement in the room was Miss Strasser's lips. They slowly tightened in a grimace of disapproval.

I finished my story and sat down. There was a scattering of applause cut off by the knifing stroke of Miss Strasser's voice: "I'm shocked! I asked for a true story, and you spin out a wild yarn that couldn't possibly be true. Everybody knows the wolves would have attacked you and that strange witchwoman you associate with. When are you ever going to learn to follow directions? You'd better spend some time in the cloakroom thinking about the meaning of co-operation."

As I dragged myself to the back of the classroom, Darold Dingert raised his hand. Miss Strasser called on him. He asked in mocking tones. "When they take the wolf cub back to its den, do you suppose the wolves will adopt Roger like Mowgli in the 'Jungle Books'?"

A torrent of laughter followed my final steps to the

cloakroom door. I glanced at Charlie. Tears of anger stained his cheeks. I spent my time thinking about how much I hated Miss Strasser.

A month later, Gletha and I returned the healed cub to the spot in the forest from which we'd rescued him. We were aware of grey shadows in the underbrush. Gletha sang one of her strange, reassuring songs. We stepped back and watched the mother wolf move cautiously toward her baby. She licked it roughly from head to foot, removing all human scent. We knew that the wild mother had received a splendid Mother's Day gift.

That summer Gletha and I walked by Miss Strasser's little house in Spruce Crossing. All my pent-up anger at the woman exploded. "I h-h-hope I never have to sit in a classroom with another teacher like her. I hope she'll get l-l-lost in the woods. Maybe a b-bear will eat her!"

Gletha paused and pointed to the front window. A gold star was suspended there, barely visible through the framing hollyhocks.

I was shocked. "I didn't know she'd l-l-lost someone in the w-w-war."

"Her twin brother was killed in the Battle of Guadalcanal. They lived together before he was called up."

"W-w-when was he killed?"

"Just before Mother's Day."

Tears sprang to my eyes as I remembered the long periods of hate I extended toward Miss Strasser from the cloakroom.

Gletha knelt down by me and tented me with her garments and her arms. She continued, "You never know what grief gits carried inside folks and how it shapes what they do to others. Hating folks never does much to heal them."

As we walked down the street, Miss Strasser rose from her garden. She had a large bunch of radishes in her hand. She smiled tentatively and said, "Why, Roger and Gletha, how nice to see you on this good, bright day. Could you use some radishes? I've got more than enough now that I'm alone."

I extended a hand to receive the gift and, without a trace of a stammer, said, "Thank you, Miss Strasser."

I remember them as the sweetest radishes I've ever eaten.

The Given Heart

The shopkeepers' wives in Spruce Crossing were *not* going to teach Daily Vacation Bible School at the tiny Lakeshore Church of Jesus Risen this year. The school, always the summer's highlight, would be taught by some very special guests. The kingdom of God was to be revealed to boys and girls, grades one through six, by students in training at St. Paul Bible Institute in the Twin Cities.

After a great deal of conflict among those in charge, it was decided that a bus should be sent out through the forest offering free transportation to the "pulpwooders' kids." Emil Larson, at the Sign of the Flying Red Horse, who notoriously overcharged everybody for everything, was willing to salve his conscience by filling the bus with gas each day "out of my love for Jesus and the children," as he put it.

The students from St. Paul Bible Institute all had conversion quotas they needed to fill. It was felt by the town folk that the timberland kids carried a particularly heavy load of depravity and would be ideal candidates for the ministrations of the guests from the big city—and the St. Paul students would have plenty of opportunity to fill their quotas.

A vast gulf separated the kids from the lumber camps and the kids from the town. The latter lived in houses—not tarpaper shacks. They had access to indoor plumbing and could bathe daily rather than on the traditional Saturday night. The most telling distinction was in the matter of clothing. Each fall many of our mothers would take us into town to the church rummage sale. Some of the ladies behind the tables, laden with castoffs, would look down on us with disdain. When worn shirts would be held up to us to check for near-fit, a word of caution was proffered: "Now, don't hold that shirt too close. We wouldn't want it to get dirty now, would we?" Some of us hated to go into town, fearing that a garment's former owner would walk by with a collection of cronies, give one hard stare and then shout, "Look, he's wearing one of my old shirts that I got tired of. Sure do feel sorry for the shirt having to walk around on the back of that stinky kid."

Be that as it may, it was decided that we could, indeed, be all thrown together to spend a week singing in happy harmony, "I've Got the Love of Jesus, Love of Jesus Down in My Heart." There was some speculation that there might be fights between the disparate factions when the pulpwooders unloaded from the bus. Heavy dependence was placed on the skills of reconciliation sure to be possessed by the students from St. Paul Bible Institute.

Word about the Bible School and the free bus spread throughout Bear Run Township. My father felt that my time would be much more profitably spent weeding the garden, trapping pocket gophers and picking berries. He had never been a devotee of institutional religion. My mother thought it might be good for me. I saw it as a means of escaping, for a few brief moments, my father's terrible anger. I knew there would be conflict with the town kids—but at least it would be different.

Before making a final decision as to my attendance, I went to consult with Gletha. Having reviewed the Church of Jesus Risen's generous proposition, I left myself open for questions. She looked at me out of those pools of darkness which were her eyes: "Rogee, why do you want to go into town for a week and listen to all those empty words about the love of Jesus when there's all that hate whirling around you? You know there's some that don't want you there."

"Maybe I want to do it just to have a week free from hearing you call me Rogee."

"That's a crazy reason. You got any others?"

"They promised to tell us a lot of stories about God and

Jesus. I've always liked stories."

"We can listen to God's voice and God's stories in the loon's call on Old Lady Slough."

"Aw, Gletha, don't be dumb. That's a scary sound that don't have nothin' to do with God."

"Everything's got somethin' to do with God," she said as she stared through the grimy kitchen window at the sunlight on the forest floor patterned by pine boughs.

"Well, maybe they'll teach me about that kind of stuff so I'll know it better."

She turned her stare on me. "You don't learn about that kind of stuff unless you travel deep inside it. Them folk at the Church of Jesus Risen tend to dance on the top of their own words."

"Well, I think I'm goin' anyway. I'll tell you what, Gletha. They always make lots of things at those vacation Bible schools. I'll make you somethin' extra nice."

"You needn't bother. Last year when they came out on Sunday afternoon and had classes and preaching in Bear Run School, you made me something nice—a clamshell painted red with 'FOR GOD SO LOVED THE WORLD' spelled out on it with alphabet macaroni. Old Deacon Tolliver let it be known that I wasn't welcome in the services 'cause I cast spells and cursed folk and their livestock. I wish them people would hang their holy words in their hearts instead of on their walls."

I left her staring out of the window at the late-afternoon shadows. She didn't even seem to hear the discomfort in the bleats of the goats as they waited around the milking stump. I glanced back just as I stepped through the door. I saw a tear on her cheek.

The next morning we all gathered at Bear Run Store where the bus from town was to pick us up. Dilly Fenn took charge immediately. "Listen, everybody. I think we'd better divide up our responsibilities if we're going to survive these little religious expeditions into town. My cousin was out from there yesterday, and he'd been with a gang of boys who were planning how they were going to knock the shit out of us the minute we got off the bus. They decided that they'd let Robert Ranke lead off for their side while the rest of them distracted the teachers by doin' the good stuff. Now, when we get to town, you girls handle joinin' in the singin' and the prayin', and I'll direct you guys in the fightin'."

In the distance we could hear the clanking of the dilapidated bus as it labored up Grey Goose Hill. Dilly Fenn had a sixth sense that Uncle Tim, the bus driver who came for us during the school year, would not be alone. He guessed that one of the visitors from St. Paul Bible Institute might well be along. Dilly wanted us all to make an unforgettable first impression so that maybe, if they saw how good we were, we wouldn't have to do all the required "holy junk." He formed us into two unaccustomed lines—boys in one and girls in the other. He set us all to singing, as loudly as possible, the only chorus we knew: "Jesus Loves Me."

As the bus came to a halt in the parking lot, it was easy to see that Dilly's hunch had been exactly right. Uncle Tim opened the bus door to reveal the skinniest young man we'd ever seen. "Jesus Loves Me" almost stopped in the midst of our further noticing his flaming red hair, thick gold-rimmed glasses, preacherly black suit and the large black Bible which he extended in one hand as he cautiously picked his way down the narrow bus steps, looking for all the world like an exorcist about to dissolve a vampire. He stared for a moment at the rag-tag collection of kids. Then he addressed us in a voice that trembled at the edge of extinction: "Boys and girls, my name is Thaddeus Huddlestory. You may call me Huddle—or-or-or even Hud."

The ensuing long moment of silence was finally broken by Dilly, "Why, thank you, MISTER Huddlestory, but my ma would skin me alive if I ever called anybody such as you by a nickname, even if you asked me to."

Again, Dilly led off with "Jesus Loves Me" in his clear, on-pitch soprano. We all followed him, physically and vocally. The boys even stood aside and let the girls mount the bus steps first. Thaddeus Huddlestory was rooted to his spot in the parking lot, shifting his great black Bible from hand to hand. The only thing exorcised at the moment was his hope of filling his conversion quota from the seemingly perfect collection of spiritual paragons which had preceded him.

Uncle Tim sat for a moment sizing up the situation. An inveterate chewer of tobacco, he leaned from his seat toward the open door and unerringly aimed a rich brown stream in the direction of a rock to the left of our would-be mentor. A mere shadow of a mist from the expert marksmanship clouded the immaculate shine of Thaddeus' black shoes. The sound of the splat shocked him back to the present moment, and he scrambled aboard just as Dilly (who had been conducting us from the aisle behind Uncle Tim) issued a cut-off to the final chorus. Turning to the visitor from St. Paul Bible Institute, he ushered him with an elaborate gesture to the nearest empty two-person bench. Thaddeus Huddlestory sat by the window. Dilly Fenn slid in beside him and folded in his lap his great fists which were more familiar with pugilistics than piety.

Uncle Tim ground the bus's tired gears. Soon we were semi-coasting down Grey Goose Hill and into the half-hour ride toward Spruce Crossing.

Thaddeus' ears began to match his hair as he sensed thirteen pairs of eyes grilling into the back of his head. His fingernails turned white as he gripped the Word of God in his lap. He glanced nervously to his left and caught the fourteenth pair of deceivingly mild blue eyes staring up at him.

Dilly asked, "Mr. Huddlestory, would it be possible for me to have a look at that fine Bible you've got in your lap?"

Thaddeus released it reluctantly as his fingernails regained their normal color. He queried, "What is your name, my boy?"

"Dilly Fenn."

"There must be more to it than that."

"There is—but if you knew it all, you might accidentally call me by it and I'd have to slug you."

Thaddeus blanched. His body automatically tried to burrow itself into the steel side of the bus. He stammered, "S-s-slug me? Why?"

"It's a promise I made to the whole world. And I think it says somewhere in this here Bible that you ought to keep promises you make—even them you make to yerself."

On Dilly's lap, the worn Bible fell open to Psalm 1. The facing page was resplendent with an engraving of Gustave Dore's "Praying Hands." Dilly shaped his hands together in the classic position. The early morning summer sunlight cast their image on the picture in shadowed exactness. For once in his life, Dilly Fenn was enjoined with greatness.

A half hour later the bus rattled through the unpaved rutted streets of Spruce Crossing. Uncle Tim pulled into the parking lot of the Lakeside Church of Jesus Risen. The sunlight glittered off Pine Lake. Baptismal Cove was glassy smooth as if waiting for a candidate for glory from the dusty bus.

They *were* waiting for us. Standing in a tight line, the town boys, led by overgrown Robert Ranke, were ready to attack. The girls were confidently ranged on the church steps. They knew that they had a veritable unbeatable Goliath in Robert. Dilly ducked and scooted down the aisle to the back of the bus as Uncle Tim pulled the vehicle just past the waiting "townies." Our girls quickly headed for the exit, drawing the attention of the waiting boys. They were closely followed by Thaddeus Huddlestory. As they moved, Letty Miller led off with "Amazing Grace." As they quickly descended the steps, Dilly popped open the rear emergency exit. Grabbing the bar above the door, he swung out and unerringly aimed his heels at Robert's head. Robert dropped to the dirt as if someone had cut the strings of a giant puppet.

There were cries from the church steps. Thaddeus, having stepped quickly to the head of the processional, was singing lustily along with the maidens from the pulpwood camps, blissfully unaware of the Armageddon about to transpire at the rear of the bus.

While Dilly was in mid-air, the rest of the boys made their move. I sat frozen, alone in my seat, afraid of the implications of involvement. Like savages dropping from ancient cliffs, they dropped from the emergency exit—one aimed at each town kid in the line. The townies never had a chance. The forest boys ground their faces in the soft dust and twisted arms painfully behind backs. There were muttered cries of "Uncle" from the stupefied village dwellers. As one man, Dilly and his cohorts rose, and in double-step joined the singing processional. I snuck off the bus and fell in at the end. The victims rose slowly, clothes dust-saturated, some faces streaked with tears. The last to move was Robert Ranke. He sat in the soft, dry earth, shaking his head dazedly, a thin trail of blood flowing from the corner of his mouth as if a tooth had been dislodged. His troops fell in around their leader to protect him from the indignity of being observed by the enemy. They got him to his feet. There was a flurry as they brushed each other off and began moving reluctantly toward the church. Uncle Tim, the silent observer of the fracas, aimed a last stream of tobacco juice after the retreating enemy, ground the gears of the bus and drove back toward the town.

As the triumphant processional snaked into the church, "Amazing Grace" came to an end. In the distance, a piano picked up a new tune. It sounded like "Twinkle, Twinkle Little Star." We stepped into the sanctuary and were assailed by the smell of decaying hymnals. Then we saw her: brilliant red hair shining in the light, high-necked white blouse, a smile welcoming us to the front pews. Thaddeus Huddlestory, still not missing half the town contingent, introduced his assistant from St. Paul Bible Institute, Miss Maryjeanne McGuthrie. He underscored the word "assistant," leaving no doubt in anyone's mind who was in charge. She continued to play "Twinkle, Twinkle" with full-scale variations as the introduction proceeded. She then matched a set of words to the familiar music:

> Jesus Christ, the Truth, the Way,
> In thy name we meet today,
> Meet to read thy gracious Word,
> Meet to hear of Christ the Lord.
>
> From this hour, we anew,
> Seek thy holy will to do,
> Give to thee each youthful heart,
> And from thee no more depart.

As the second stanza began, the town boys skulked into the back of the sanctuary. Without missing a beat, Thaddeus Huddlestory rushed down the aisle, fluttered around them and shepherded them to the main body of scholars. Dilly Fenn, sitting on the end of an aisle, turned and caught Robert Ranke's eye and held it for a long moment. Robert dropped his head in shame.

The tension was broken when Thaddeus was inspired to have a contest between the boys and the girls to see who could sing the loudest:

> The B-I-B-L-E,
> Yes, that's the Book for me.
> I'll stand alone of the Word of God:
> The B-I-B-L-E.

Maryjeanne McGuthrie finished her stint at the piano and moved to Thaddeus' side. Her cool beauty, shining through a make-up-less complexion and cool smile, mesmerized every boy. Every girl released a bit of sinful envy.

Together, they outlined what was obviously going to be the high point of the entire week: **The Great Bible Verse Memorization Contest**. Two teams would be formed. Each would choose a captain. All team members would memorize as many verses as possible. Thaddeus and Maryjeanne would tally verses through the week. At the closing exercises in the presence of all the parents, the captains would square off against each other. There would be two prizes: one for the winning team and one for the victorious captain.

Robert Ranke raised his head quickly. Here was a way to vindicate himself and the other victims. Everybody knew the pulpwood kids were just plain dumb. The contest was made to order for the more sophisticated denizens of metropolis. His overbearing voice rang out, "Mr. Thaddeus—Miss Maryjeanne—why don't we divide between country and town? We're about equal in terms of numbers."

Thaddeus and Maryjeanne smiled at each other. They seemed to do a lot of that.

Maryjeanne responded, "What an absolutely splendid idea. Why don't the country children pass to the basement where we're going to have crafts next and choose a captain, while the rest of you remain here and make your choice. Will the first group please turn, stand and pass?"

We discovered that turning in the pews was extremely awkward, but we did manage to stand and pass. As Dilly moved around Robert, the latter muttered under his breath, "You're dead in the water on this one!" Dilly walked on without looking at him.

When we arrived in the dark little room beneath the Church of Jesus Risen, replete with the smell of endless potlucks,

Dilly quickly organized us in his usual fashion as Maryjeanne stood by helplessly.

"Okay! We may get walloped. All the town kids have to do is lay around and memorize their stupid Bibles. We've got wood to cut, cows to milk and blueberries to pick. Do what you can. We destroyed them this morning. Girls, it will be pretty much up to you."

LaVonne Lafferty responded, "Aunt Theo taught us to memorize stuff real good. We can maybe do better than you think, Dilly Fenn. But who can be captain? I hear that Robert Ranke is not only the toughest kid in town but also the smartest."

Dilly laughed wryly, "The same cannot be said for me on both counts."

He turned to me, "Roger, you memorize the fastest of anybody."

There was an embarrassed silence. Everybody in the group knew the truth of Dilly's statement. They also knew that my terrible stammer would not allow me to get up in front of all the parents on Friday night and challenge Robert Ranke. They were all terrified of such a setting. Finally I muttered, "I'll d-d-d-do it." The group cheered my willingness, but realized the contest was probably lost on both counts.

In mid-afternoon I climbed off the bus and headed for Gletha's shack. Uncle Pud's stentorian snores came from behind the burlap curtain when I opened the door. She was cooking down blueberries for jam.

"Gletha, I got myself into a terrible fix."

She looked at me for a long moment. "And what's new about that? What did you go and do this time?"

"There's gonna' be a big contest learning Bible verses and the Bear Run kids are against the Spruce Crossing kids and I'm supposed to be the one who stands up against Robert Ranke on Friday when the parents come for the closing exercises and all I'll do when I get up in front of everybody is stammer. Gletha, you know you're the only one I can ever talk to without stuttering away. I also need to borrow your Bible so I can learn a whole lot of the Holy Word of God."

Gletha pulled the worn volume of Sacred Writ from the shelf and sat down at the table. She made a circle with her thumbs and forefingers over the cover. She sat in silence, her eyes closed, her lips moving. It was one of those moments when I knew I shouldn't interrupt. She opened her eyes. I asked, "Gletha, what were you doing just now?"

"I was putting myself in touch with the wholeness."

"Well, I sure need to put myself in touch with something too."

I put my fingers and thumbs in a smaller circle over hers. I closed my eyes. She lowered her head until her cheek touched mine. All I felt was warmth and multi-colored circles of wholeness spinning wildly in my mind's eye.

She lifted her head. I removed my hands. She opened the Book to a special section at the back that seemed to be about Bible verses. Together we began to make a plan.

Daily Vacation Bible School progressed in relative peace. Without knowing it, Maryjeanne McGuthrie and Thaddeus Huddlestory had moved the basic battle from the parking lot to the classroom. Each morning, while we did things like assist St. Francis of Assisi by making suet and peanut butter balls for the birds, Thaddeus and Maryjeanne would be surrounded by those who wanted to recite contest verses. Thaddeus kept the score for the boys and girls from Spruce Crossing while Maryjeanne calculated totals for the Bear Run team. No one was to know the outcome until the evening of the closing program. Those two young Bible scholars, Robert and Dilly, often smiled at each other across the classroom.

Each day I'd dash for Gletha's just as soon as I hopped off the bus. We'd gather herbs and berries, cook up salves and syrups and milk the goats at moonrise. Through all these activities, Gletha taught me verse after verse until I lost track of just how many I'd memorized. I was somehow beyond worry.

Excitement reigned supreme on Friday. All projects were being finished so that they might be displayed for admiring parents and siblings. The Bible verses on clam shells were properly drying. All the pulpwooder kids were haunted by the possibility that the townies were mounting a special last day of school attack.

They must have been saving our ultimate whipping for the Bible verse contest. Not a cross word was spoken as our group began the long march across the playground to the bus. We made it without incident. At that point, however, leering jibes were shouted. Robert led off with, "Tonight, you'll be d-e-e-e-stroyed."

Disembarking from the bus, I raced to Gletha's. "Gletha, I'm not ready for tonight. I'm gonna' look dumber than usual."

"The more you talk about your fear, the more real it gets. Now sit down and let's do a little work." She pulled the worn volume off the shelf, and we continued the process she'd begun four days before.

My father was out of his darkness and decided that he really did want to go to the program. My mother and I were stunned—but pleased. I asked him if Gletha could ride with us, and he reluctantly agreed to spending three hours in her presence. When I presented her with this wonderful opportunity, she stopped me with, "Rogee, you know they won't let me into their church 'cause they got a lot of strange ideas about the ways I befriend the Spirit."

"But, Gletha, I'll just tell them you're my guest. Since I'm gonna' be on the platform, I really need you there. Otherwise, I'll just fall apart."

She reluctantly agreed. At six o'clock we climbed into the old rattletrap Chevy and drove into Spruce Crossing. An incredible harvest moon was edging up out of the distant lake. For a moment the Church of Jesus Risen was shadowed across it looking for all the world like it was going to rise with the heavenly orb.

My father parked the car at the edge of the crowded lot. We recognized a number of the vehicles belonging to our township neighbors. As we moved toward the church steps, old Deacon Tolliver, his beer belly hanging over his belt, started down toward us. His raspy voice hatcheted through the sultry July night, "You git out of here, witchlady. We're all good Christian folk in here, and we don't allow any witch wimmin inside."

My father and mother lowered their eyes in embarrassment. I started to stammer out an angry response. I felt a light touch on my shoulder—and then I caught a glimpse of Gletha disappearing into the forest. Her grey cloths flowed out from her like soft bat wings in the light evening breeze off the lake.

Deacon Tolliver, a look of triumph on his face at having won a battle with the devil herself, walked back into the church. We reluctantly followed.

Inside, we discovered the pulpwooder families occupying the back pews. The townsfolk had walked over early to claim the best seats. Rumors had flowed throughout Spruce Crossing that the pulpwooders' kids were going to be shown up for the dunces they really were.

Thaddeus Huddlestory and Maryjeanne McGuthrie kept the program moving. Each class sang some songs and recited short, pious poems. However, everyone seemed to be focused on the major event to come.

I began to feel sick to my stomach. Thaddeus called Robert and me to the front. As I dragged myself up the aisle, the lower panel of a stained glass window—the one showing Jesus suffering the little children to come to him—was open. There, leaning against a pine tree in the moonlight where she could see and hear everything, was Gletha. Something like a diamond glistened on her cheek—the afterglow of the pain from Deacon Tolliver's scathing words. My nausea left me instantly. I squared my shoulders and marched determinedly up onto the platform.

Thaddeus Huddlestory assumed the voice of a ring announcer heralding a Joe Lewis boxing match. "We now come to the featured attraction of the evening: **The Great Bible Verse Memorization Contest**. On my right, representing the village of Spruce Crossing, is that fine young budding Bible scholar, Robert Ranke. On my left, representing Bear Run Township, is Roger Robbennolt. Now most of us know that Roger has a bad stammer. We'll have to be a little patient as the evening moves ahead." His tone was so patronizing that I was on the one hand humiliated and on the other hand angry enough to beat anybody at anything.

Thaddeus Huddlestory reviewed the rules. Each of us would recite a verse. The other would respond until there were no more verses of Sacred Writ available inside either of us. A coin was flipped, and it was ascertained that Robert would go first.

Robert's face was suffused by a self-confident sneer. He looked at me and spat out, "Jesus wept," the shortest verse in the Bible. Then he gave me a long vanquishing grin. Some of the Spruce Crossing adults broke out in laughter. There was much back and knee slapping. The folk from Bear Run Township sat frozen in place, resigned to one more defeat at the hands of their more sophisticated town peers.

I looked out the window. Gletha was staring back at me. I decided to try to intimidate him off the stage. And so I tore loose:

> Esther 8:9—the longest verse in the Bible: "Then were the king's scribes called at that time in the third month, that is, the month Sivan, on the three and twentieth day thereof; and it was written according to all that Mordecai commanded unto the Jews, and to the lieutenants, and the deputies and the rulers of the provinces which are from India unto Ethiopia, a hundred twenty and seven provinces, unto every province according to the writing thereof, and unto every people after their language, and to the Jews according to their writing, and according to their language."

I had raced through the text at breakneck speed without a trace of a stammer. The pulpwooder families broke into wild applause. The children cheered. Deacon Tolliver stormed down the aisle and shouted the celebrants into silence, "Remember where you all are. I realize you're not here very often, but in this place we always try to show God a little respect." He returned to his guard post in the rear of the church.

Thaddeus Huddlestory motioned for Robert to continue. He ran out Genesis 1:13: "And the evening and the morning were the third day."

I decided to give him back Ezra 7:21—the only verse in the Bible which has all the letters of the alphabet except "J":

> "And I, even I, Artaxerxes the king, do make a decree to all the treasurers which are beyond the river, that whatsoever Ezra the priest, the scribe of the law of the God of heaven, shall require of you, it be done speedily."

This time the pulpwooders did not applaud. They stamped their feet on the worn pine floorboards. The sound echoed through the basement and back up into the room like the thunder of the wrath of Yahweh. Robert Ranke's face glistened with sickly sweat. His mother, seated in the front row, sent his little sister hightailing to the basement to fetch him a glass of Kool-Aid.

Thaddeus smiled nervously at Robert, who finally managed to stammer out Genesis 1:19: "And the evening and the morning were the forth day."

I looked out the window, and Gletha smiled her mysterious smile and nodded. The message from the sidelines was clear:

> Daniel 4: 37—the only verse in the Bible with all the letters of the alphabet except "Q": "Now, I, Nebuchadnezzar, praise and extol and honor the King of heaven, all whose works are truth, and his ways judgment..."

I paused for a moment, looked at Robert with an intensely hostile stare and raised my voice dramatically as I finished the verse: " '...and those that walk in pride he is able to abase.' "

A roar of laughter went up from the occupants of the rear pews. Deacon Tolliver again shouted for "Silence, in the name of the Lord!"

Robert came up with a few more "days," some of the shorter "begats" and some scattered *bon mots* from Proverbs. I specialized in Paul's convoluted sentences and theological obscurantism.

I was on a roll. Robert Ranke had come to the end of both his Kool-Aid and his memory bank of Holy Scriptures. I plunged on, determined to let the whole world know just what had been pumped into me in the forest clearings and on the goatshed milking stool. As I moved through verse after verse, I saw Gletha standing taller in the harvest light. She held up a circled thumb and finger—and through the circle I saw the moon and focused on it—and further reservoirs of knowledge opened. After ten minutes, with the audience awed by the stammering pulpwooder kid flawlessly repeating inerrant words, Thaddeus Huddlestory began to wave his Bible at me.

I waved back—and kept on reciting.

It finally occurred to me that Thaddeus was trying to get me to stop. I was transformed and felt, for a moment, a terrible freedom. Then I saw Maryjeanne McGuthrie move quickly to the piano. She began to play "Twinkle, Twinkle Little Star" and encouraged the nearest children to begin singing:

> Jesus Christ, the Truth, the Way,
> In thy name we meet today.

However, everyone was mesmerized by the flow of verses.

Finally, Deacon Tolliver moved down the aisle with a sickly smile on his face. He put his hand on my shoulder. The seam of my shirt was torn. I could feel the cold claminess of his touch. The stream of my words was damned up by revulsion.

"Well, well, well. Isn't it good that each of the teams of our little Christian seekers should win a prize tonight. The Spruce Crossing team wins for the most individual verses learned by the team members together. The Bear Run team takes pride in their captain's fine victory."

Maryjeanne McGuthrie moved from her place at the piano to Thaddeus' side where they both shifted their weight from foot to foot, looking uncomfortable. Thaddeus again waved his Bible weakly. Deacon Tolliver stopped his brief victory paean to acknowledge Thaddeus: "You wanted to add a word of testimony, did you, Brother Huddlestory?"

It was Thaddeus' turn to stammer, "N-N-N-No, sir. I n-n-n-needed to add a word of correction. In the team contest, the Bear Run team was checked on 137 verses. The Spruce Crossing team was checked on 121."

Pandemonium ensued at the back of the church as the pulpwooders leapt to their feet with rebel yells, praising God that one of their number had bested a townie and that teamwork learned on gang saw and quilting frame could win the day. The children too went wild. Dilly Fenn led our troops, circling the church with his exuberant followers. Except for his ragged clothing, he might have been David dancing before the Lord.

After two circles, the chanting children returned to their seats.

Deacon Tolliver raised his hand for silence. I looked at Gletha. She was staring down toward the lake rippling in the moonlight. Her soft grey cloths were flowing in the breeze. Then, she turned to me once more and smiled a beatific smile.

Deacon Tolliver cleared his throat loudly and proclaimed, "Ladies and gentlemen, we're right proud to have in our midst tonight a little walking Bible. And now, Roger, I want you to consider the most important decision in your life. I want everybody within the sound of my voice to bow his head in prayer that this dear boy makes the right decision."

Every head bowed except Gletha's.

Deacon Tolliver droned on, "Young man, I want you, at this very moment, to give your heart to Jesus."

I looked at the exiled goatlady leaning against the pine tree in the moonlight. I turned to the huge old man and spat out my words with no trace of a stammer, "I ain't ever gonna' give my heart to your kind of Jesus—because long ago I gave my heart to Gletha."

Every head in the church jerked up simultaneously. I squared my shoulders and marched down the center aisle and out the door. Gletha was waiting for me at the bottom of the steps. More diamonds seemed to be glistening on her cheeks. She gave me a long, wordless embrace. Releasing me, she threw a fold of the soft grey cloth around my shoulders. We seemed to float to the lake shore.

Gletha said, "Listen deeply. You'll hear God speakin'."

From the center of the lake came the loon's cry.

Charlie and the Beaver

The deacons met around a shaky table in the odoriferous basement of the Lakeside Church of Jesus Risen. A severe problem presented itself. At the annual ice cream social, just before the commencement of Daily Vacation Bible School, Pelius McDowell, their beloved minister of twenty-one years, had keeled over dead from a heart attack. At Corner's Corner Cafe, Mattie Corner was heard to remark (possibly out of a bit of jealousy) that she suspected their slightly more than pleasingly plump pastor had succumbed to a fatal combination of Myrtle Givens' lemon chiffon pie, accompanied by a side dish of Patsy Martin's blackberry brandy ice cream topped with a generous dollop of Marjorie Blanchard's famous gooseberry preserves.

Whatever the reasons for the good Reverend Pelius' demise, the deacons wrestled with the problem of who should continue the proclamation of the Good News in his stead. Then someone remarked that the fine young man from the St. Paul Bible Institute, Thaddeus Huddlestory, was doing a fine job with the children in the Bible School. He'd finished his course of study in the city. Perhaps he could be prevailed upon to continue as pastor.

There was some concern that Thaddeus was unmarried— but others speculated that his single state was fairly easily transformed. Maryjeanne McGuthrie, his assistant for the week, seemed never to take her eyes off him. At that very moment glorious sounds wafted their way to the dank basement as Thaddeus and Maryjeanne rehearsed the choruses with which they would edify the children on the morrow. Maryjeanne's piano runs were simply mesmerizing in their complexity. It was decided that "strike while the iron's hot" should be the order of the day. Someone was sent to summon the unsuspecting pair to the diaconal tribunal.

An hour later, after much joshing from their elders and blushes from the young people, it was ascertained that they did indeed plan to marry. The date could be brought forward to a couple of weeks after the close of Bible School. They would be proud to serve the Lord in the midst of such fine folk and such co-operative children. Thaddeus did confess, a bit shakily, that he still hadn't quite gotten used to the wilderness after all his years in the big city. He hoped he could avoid meeting face-to-face the bear and the timber wolves and the unidentified beasts which stalked his dreams. The meeting closed with a prayer of thanksgiving that the Holy Spirit had sent an answer to their corporate needs with such rapidity.

Before progressing any further, I've got to tell you about my friend Charlie. He lived with an absolutely enormous woman whom everyone in Bear Run Township called "Big Mama." Nobody knew for sure if he really was her son, but it didn't make that much difference. Sometimes a wizened little man would appear for a few days. He had a huge lump on his lip which never went away after a slab tossed from a sawmill blade smashed into his mouth. Again, nobody was quite sure if that was Charlie's dad—but nobody bothered to inquire.

Charlie and Big Mama were awfully poor. There were days when Charlie came to school with a little lard spread on a slice of bread decorated with a smidgen of cinnamon. I always tried to share a sugar-and-molasses cookie—or even an early radish from the garden. His clothes consisted of patches rudely sewn over patches.

We shared a seat on the school bus. His raggedness and my stammer made us both outcasts and the butt of everybody's derision on the playground.

Charlie had one skill I deeply envied. Charlie loved the water and could swim like an otter. Sometimes Gletha took us both with her when she went into the forest to gather herbs. If it was warm by the time we got to Fever Pond, Charlie would be out of his clothes in an instant and sliding through the water more easily than he walked on dry land. I once asked Gletha quietly, "What if someone came by and saw Charlie out there bare-naked? Wouldn't he be terribly punished?"

"Ain't nothin' wrong with the naked human body if it's being used in beauty. And there ain't nothin' more beautiful than that boy cavorting in the water."

After that, I always slipped off my clothes and waded in the shallows. Most folk had done a good job of making me feel useless and ugly. I needed to be beautiful too. The loons and the mallards swam nearby in sun-dappled loveliness, making us feel at one with them.

I remember the day when we three climbed into the back seat of my father's rattletrap Chevy and headed into Spruce Crossing for some "necessities." Dad was out of his darkness and had gotten paid for some pulpwood cutting. While Mom shopped for flour and sugar, Gletha, Charlie and I headed for Tamarack Creek which ran into Baptismal Cove. We'd heard tell that beavers were putting the finishing touches on a new dam.

Arriving on the creek bank, we discovered the dam in place with its placid pond glinting in the warm July sunlight. Its surface was only occasionally disturbed by the soft "plunk" of a feeding northern pike.

Charlie was disappointed. "I wanted to see the beavers workin'."

Gletha smiled at him for a moment and then began to sing one of her strange songs. The melody embraced wind and rustling birch leaves and full moonlight even in the presence of the midday sun. Something deep inside Charlie felt the song. He stepped to a large flat rock slightly submerged at the pond's edge. He began to move slowly, sinuously in a dance of light and shadow. As his feet shattered the water's surface, the harsh sun rays glittered on the flying spray. It looked like he danced in liquid fire.

The beavers heard the song. One after another, six sleek heads broke the surface of the water and seemed suspended in a semi-circle focused on the melody and the boy. A seventh rich brown body appeared closer to shore, its great white teeth glowing in the sunlight like jewels against the blue water. It too began to move to the rhythm of Gletha's song. Boy and beaver were dancing together—each in his own element. Then, without interrupting the flow, Charlie slipped off his overalls and knifed into the water, scarcely disturbing its tranquility.

The pace of Gletha's melody quickened. Together, beast and boy arced through the water with a kind of ecstatic joy. It was often difficult to tell which was which as two brown heads sliced along the surface. Caught up in the scene, I leapt to the rock vacated by Charlie and began to move as he had moved. I desperately wanted to slip out of my clothes and complete the three-way ballet of freedom. But we were too close to town. If my father should come upon us, I'd know the whip's lash for "shaming him" with my craziness.

The moment was shattered by the squawk of the Chevy's horn calling us back to the mundane world of loading sacks of chicken feed and heading back toward the gathering darkness of Bear Run Township. Charlie and the beaver nose-nuzzled in parting. He swam to the flat rock, shook himself and drew on his overalls. The animals listened to the dying echoes of the song—then disappeared.

For the rest of the summer Charlie begged rides with us to Spruce Crossing whenever "necessities" were again required. It always seemed that I had to help with townside errands. Charlie would immediately disappear. A blast of the Chevy's horn would draw him back. His shaggy, rich brown hair would be wet. A strange deep peace would radiate from his eyes.

Late August, Big Mama got a job in Spruce Crossing as a barmaid in Pine Mountain Pool Hall and Beverage Service. The shack in the country was exchanged for a shack in town. Rumor had it that she partook a little too heavily of the hospitality offered by the lumberjacks. Charlie often reported that Big Mama was terribly sick in the morning. I was lonely. There was nobody to sit with on the long school bus ride to town since Bear Run School had been closed by consolidation. We got to spend lunch hour together. Even though Big Mama had a steady source of income, there seemed to be no improvement in his fare of larded bread with its touch of cinnamon. I continued to share whatever appeared in my lunch box by the way of scrambled egg sandwiches and apple pie.

Indian summer was upon us. The autumn heat held for days. Desultory students yawned their way through tedious classroom exercises. Charlie informed me that Big Mama had suddenly become really concerned about his soul. She had never had him baptized. She'd arranged to have him dunked in Baptismal Cove following next Sunday's eleven o'clock service at the Lakeside Church of Jesus Risen.

Charlie wanted me and Gletha there with him in the worst way. After our experience at the Vacation Bible School program, there was no way we'd come to morning worship. However, we might hide ourselves in the thick hazelnut bushes that grew right down to the water's edge and watch him become a new son of the living God. At least that's what Thaddeus Huddlestory had assured him he would be after coming up out of the water of Baptismal Cove. Considering his years of uncertain parenting, it all sounded pretty good to Charlie.

Gletha had sold some extra goatmilk that week because Claude Denning had developed a bad ulcer. She convinced my Uncle Pud that they could afford a bit of gas for the battered little truck. She also persuaded him he could stay awake long enough to drive to town and could take a long nap there before driving home again.

We left early on Sunday morning. The ancient vehicle sputtered as we climbed Grey Goose Hill, but transit to Spruce Crossing was miraculously achieved. We parked on a rutted side street not far from the church. Pud immediately slumped snoring over the wheel. Gletha and I headed for the lake shore and situated ourselves to be near the sacramental spot and also where we could see the worshipers going in and out of the Lakeside Church of Jesus Risen.

The September heat was oppressive. Men arriving for worship removed their dark suitcoats as they climbed the steps with their fanning wives to be greeted by the dampish welcoming hand of Thaddeus Huddlestory flanked by the ever-blushing Maryjeanne. Thaddeus, unable to bring himself to descend to a state of undignified shirtsleevedness, was carefully clad in full three-piece clerical black. Rivers of perspiration ran down the surface of his thick gold-rimmed glasses.

As the service progressed, the entire countryside was loudly aware that we were all to be "Washed in the Blood of the Lamb." Then Thaddeus' earnest exhortations shot through with condemnation and cold comfort echoed through the pines. Gletha hummed her own hymn to a slightly more caring God who gave us the gift of hazelnuts to salve our hunger as noon approached.

Baptisms at the Lakeside Church of Jesus Risen had followed the same pattern for as long as anybody could remember. The entire congregation processed the five-hundred yards from the church steps to the water's edge singing "Shall We Gather at the River." They were always headed up by Gracie Stiles, the choir's lead soprano. This had been the pattern for nigh unto seventy years. At ninety-one, Gracie's arthritis was such that the processional moved very slowly, but her voice still carried a definitive note of authority. I thought it was a dumb song since they were coming to a cove, not a river, but such niceties seemed to escape the congregation.

Thaddeus, anxious to get the job done, burst through the church door, Charlie in tow. His only change of apparel had been the donning of immense wading boots during the closing hymn. The inordinate length of his legs thus clad would allow him to wade out to a sufficient depth to dunk Charlie before the placid waters of the cove dampened his crotch. Gletha chuckled deeply as the black-clad ecclesiastical apparition clumped toward us, a hand clamped tightly on Charlie's shoulder. She began to sing a wild, slow melody indistinguishable from the wind in the leaves and the babble of Tamarack Creek as it freed itself from the captivity of the beavers' dam.

Inside the Lakeside Church of Jesus Risen, the congregation had begun to sing its marching song. Gracie Stiles' strident soprano soared out. Gletha and I knew that at any moment now they would emerge through the front double doors of the church.

As pastor and candidate reached the lake shore, Thaddeus bent to adjust a wader strap. In that instant Charlie skinned out of his ragged overalls and shirt. He stood there, his perfect body golden in the autumn light framed by the reds, oranges and yellows of the oaks, maples and poplars which lined the cove.

Thaddeus straightened up, turned—and saw Charlie. He gasped. As his glance fell to Charlie's "privates," he reddened and cried out in a strangled voice, "Boy, what have you done?"

Charlie sensed his discomfiture with wide-eyed wonder and replied, "You told me I was to go under the water while my sins were washed away. I always take off my clothes when I go in the water."

Thaddeus thundered, "You are not going to stand there, your filthy body buck-naked before God and his people who are about to come through that church door any minute."

"My body ain't filthy. Big Mama made me even wash behind my ears before she went back to bed where she's terrible sick. 'Sides, I don't think them ragged overalls and torn shirt make me any more acceptable to God. Gletha always says our bodies are beautiful just as God made 'em, if we use 'em right."

Thaddeus' facial coloration shaded from red to angry white as he spat out between his teeth, "You will learn the fear of the Lord!" In an unexpected instant, his hand lashed out and slapped Charlie resoundingly across the face. Charlie lost his balance and, as if someone had cut a puppet's strings, sunk to the sand where he sobbed quietly and began putting his overalls back on.

At the sickening sound of the blow, I leapt to go to Charlie's defense, but Gletha held me in an iron grip. Her song increased in intensity beneath the sacred chorus now emanating from the open doors as Gracie Stiles limped into view, followed by the procession of the faithful who had already learned the fear of the Lord.

Thaddeus, a great black predator, bent over Charlie and shoved him into the worn shirt, ripping it down the back in the process. He yanked Charlie to his feet. Charlie stood there before God and the approaching people clothed in ragged respectability, naked back, tears streaming down his face, a swelling, ugly red welt scarring his cheek.

Charlie turned toward the Reverend Huddlestory and spoke with quiet intensity: "If Big Mama didn't want me to do it so bad, I'd never let the likes of you put me under the water. I don't think God ever wants folk to hit folk in the name of the Father or the Son or the Holy Ghost."

Thaddeus turned to welcome the approaching congregation, a frozen smile on his face.

When everyone was in place at the lakeside, Thaddeus waded into the water with one hand gripping Charlie's shoulder. Nobody quite knew if he was guiding or leaning. When the water was mid-thigh on his waders and well above Charlie's waist, they stopped. Thaddeus began to intone the saving formula. Gletha's song shifted to a strange trill which matched the birds in the surrounding trees. A smile deepened on her face.

As Thaddeus lifted Charlie high out of the water in preparation for his "journey to the depths to be cleansed forever from your sin," it happened. A sleek brown head surfaced no more than three feet in front of the intoning pastor. Charlie's pond companion seemed to be smiling in delight, its tree-cutting incisors gleaming more broadly than usual. Thaddeus was transfixed with terror as the beast from the deep bore down upon him. He dropped the suspended Charlie with a tremendous splash, tearing the shredded shirt the rest of the way from his back.

With a scream that could be heard in the next county, Thaddeus turned and plunged awkwardly toward the shore. His cry was echoed by Maryjeanne, who implored, "Do something, somebody! The animal's attacking him!"

Deacon Tolliver expostulated, "The poor young dumb fool. It's only a beaver which won't attack nothing."

Thaddeus Huddlestory scarcely paused as he kicked off his boots and grabbed Maryjeanne around her slender waist. Together they ran across the church parking lot to their new Ford which many in the congregation thought was "too good for a preacher" but which had been given to them by their parents as a wedding gift. The astounded gathering of worshipers, now in complete disarray, began to stream after the retreating pastoral pair. As they hit the parking lot, Thaddeus roared out, turning the corner into Heartlove Street on two wheels.

Word had it later that the newlyweds packed their meager belongings and left the wilds behind forever and were never heard from again. The present confusion was compounded by the fact that Gracie Stiles had an attack of the vapors, and two of the deacons had to lock hands in a "carrying chair" to tote her back while their wives waved the complimentary fans provided by Mackin's Funeral Parlor.

In the melee, Charlie—and any concern for the state of his eternal soul—was forgotten. When he surfaced after his unexpected plunge, he came up nose to nose with his friend, the beaver. After nuzzling for a moment, the beaver swam 'round and 'round him in an obvious invitation to play follow-the-leader. Charlie treaded water for a moment, then kicked his way out of his overalls, which floated on the surface like a flat, blue water lily. He cavorted with his friend.

Some time later, after the congregation had returned to their homes to rest up from the confusion of the morning, Charlie tired of the game. He swam lazily to the shore where Gletha and I were waiting. His face was alive with the magnificent experience of freedom he'd shared with his friend. He turned to Gletha, "Gletha, do you s'pose my eternal soul is now clean in the eyes of God?"

"Charlie, your eternal soul was created clean in the eyes of God, and your body's beautiful when you use it for God's praise."

"Well, I guess I'd better be goin' to see how Big Mama's doin'. Thanks for coming. I'll never forget this day as long as I live."

Gletha and I walked through the woods, aware of three sounds woven together: Pud's snoring as he slept, still hunched over the steering wheel, the sound of the northern pike feeding in the beaver pond and the loon's song of praise to the Creator who made all things beautiful.

The Goatshed Madonna

I'll never forget sixteen-year-old Pauline Pucharski. She often came to school with bruises on her face and neck. We kids suspected that her long-sleeved blouses covered further evidence of pain. When questioned, her response was either, "The old red cow kicked me off the milk stool" or "I felled down the cellar steps." We all knew that anyone who walked to the front of the classroom like a dancer from one of the Greek vases pictured in our history book would never "felled down the cellar steps."

One day, as Dilly Fenn and I held the halves of the world together, she bent over to point to the Malay Archipelago. The sunlight reflected upward from the Polish opal and illumined an ugly purplish bruise under her chin. The imprint of the fist was clearly visible. We'd all seen her daddy stagger from the saloon in town. Sometimes he'd scream in broken English—shot through with Polish—something about "watching them burning in the ovens." It wasn't until years later that I began to suspect the roots of his agony as I read of occasional Polish workers who escaped from labor in the Nazi death camp at Treblinka.

I felt terrible for Pauline. My daddy beat my mother and me too, but somehow that was different. He usually only did it when he was sliding into one of his darknesses. We could always keep him hidden so that nobody but Gletha ever knew. I think Pauline "knew." That day, when I spotted the bruise under her chin, she caught me staring—and she looked at me with her great blue eyes and saw straight through to my pain. That afternoon Aunt Theo took Pauline home with her "to keep her company while Harry joined the timber crew in the next county over."

Nobody was too surprised when word went around Bear Run Township in mid-July that Pauline Pucharski had disappeared. Some folk said she'd "taken up" with the oldest of the "mangy Dunker boys" when he'd been home on furlough in March. There were some who thought that maybe she'd run away and joined him somewhere. However, in October the whole township stood around an open grave and watched Clive Dunker's casket, newly arrived from the South Pacific, lowered out of sight. The flag was handed to his emaciated mother. Pauline Pucharski was nowhere to be seen. As the weeks went on, the women who gathered around the quilting frames ceased to mention her.

It was Christmas Eve. I was excited. I was going to receive a single gift that holiday: a goosedown comforter. I'd watched the patchwork pieces from my old shirts and my mother's worn dresses emerge into a major work of art as the neighbor women gathered that early December. They sewed in the batting of down carefully preserved from many a season's hunt. They tried to outdo each other with the delicacy of their stitches as the quilting was completed. Gletha had secretly slipped in a dried mullein flower to "deepen down" my sleep.

Darkness came early that late-December afternoon, and a full moon shone with almost painful intensity. I approached the house from the barn, carrying two pails of still-warm milk. The milking had not taken as long as usual. The cows seemed to sense the approach of the Holy Night and remained calm as cold fingers stroked warm teats. I had not suffered the indignity of picking myself out of the manure-spattered gutter after a well-placed kick.

My mother met me at the door and reached for the pails. "You git yourself to Gletha's and spend the night. Your dad is startin' to slip into a darkness."

I stammered out, "Oh, Ma. I'm not g-g-gonna' I-leave you alone on Christmas Eve. And besides, you promised I could sleep the night for the first time under my goosedown comforter. And I intend to do just that."

My mother was adamant. "If you stay around here, you'll do some dumb thing which will set him off worse, and we'll both be beat. Now you git!"

Since I was an expert at doing dumb things which set him off, I "got." I slipped down the back cellar steps and took a jar of Ma's prize blueberry jam from the cobwebbed shelf. We'd picked the berries the day of the summer storm when I discovered that Gletha really needed me.

I moved across the moonlit, white-swathed field, a single magus carefully bearing a gift to the center of Power. The wolves were caroling in the distance. Deer rooted in the snow for corn nubbins. They didn't even run at my approach. They'd seen me pass this way so many times before. The brightest star in the night sky seemed to hover over Gletha and Pud's farmstead. I followed it in hushed silence.

As I entered their clearing, I passed the goatshed. It was eerily quiet. Then I heard a muffled cry like that of a small bird caught in an owl's talons. It seemed to come from the shed. I opened the double doors. The moonlight flooded in to illumine Pauline Pucharski stretched out on the straw, the Polish opal glowing at her throat. The goats were gathered around her like archangels on a cheap Christmas card. She was stifling cries as she clasped her rounded abdomen. She opened her eyes and stared at me wordlessly. This time I saw into the depths of her pain. I fled quickly toward Gletha's shack.

She sat in her moonlit kitchen, crooning "It Came Upon a Midnight Clear." Pud snored loudly behind the sacking curtain. I burst out, "Gletha, you got to c-come quick! Pauline Pucharski's stretched out on the straw in the goatshed. She's just laying there, moaning."

I looked down as I caught my breath and was surprised to discover that in my excitement, I was still carrying the jar of blueberry jam. I stammered out in the same shrill tones, "And here's some j-j-jam for you and Pud for Christmas."

"Rogee, stop your shouting. Don't you know nothing about 'Silent Night'?"

"If you don't stop calling me that, I'll stand here and scream all night!"

Ignoring me, she rose and wrapped herself in another layer

of her soft grey fabric. She flicked the end of it around my shoulders over my sheepskin coat. We seemed to float through the moon-silvered clearing.

When we arrived at the goatshed, Gletha said nothing. Pauline opened her eyes. Gletha looked at her from her pools of darkness and crooned a strange song which sounded more related to a loon's call than a Yuletide carol. Pauline's body began to relax.

Gletha pulled me outside and said, "There's going to be a baby born here right soon. I've got some things to get. You stay here and Joseph her."

My first instinct was to flee into the snow-laden forest. "Aw, Gletha. You mean you want me to go back in there and stay with her and hold her hand or something? Well, I'm here to tell you, I'm not gonna' do it. I don't even know who the daddy is!"

Gletha grabbed my shoulder hard, looked at me deeply and replied, "Neither did Joseph. Now you git!" She shoved me toward the goatshed door. For the second time that Christmas Eve, the word "git" had made me a reluctant journeyer.

I re-entered the shed. Pauline was calmer now. She said, "Hello, Roger."

"Hello, Pauline. Does it hurt bad?"

"I been hurt worse."

I knelt in the straw at her side. The goats moved in close around me. I was grateful for their warmth. "Where you been all this time?"

"I be hiding in the shack by Fever Pond where Old Otto deaded. He had plenty in-can food left what nobody took."

The pain struck again, and she grabbed for my hand. I was embarrassed. I'd seen baby goats born and baby calves—but this was going to be a baby! I turned my head away and closed my eyes so tightly that the star I'd noticed earlier seemed to burst into fire behind my taut lids. As the pain sharpened, I thought my fingers would break in her grasp.

I don't know how long I knelt there or when Gletha returned. I only know that I was shocked back to the present by a forceful cry and the midnight-tolling bell of the old clock in the shack echoing through the frozen air. I opened my eyes to see Gletha swaddling a wailing, obviously male infant in her soft grey cloths. She placed the baby in his mother's arms. The goats, silent until that moment, baaed a welcome.

Gletha began to formulate an immediate plan. "We've got to get Pauline and the baby to the warmest place possible. Rogee, your shack is the tightest in the township, and your daddy always keeps it hot. We'll take her there."

I didn't even bother to argue with Gletha over the hated name. I had another concern: "Take Pauline and the baby to our place? You can't take them there. Dad's going into one of his darknesses. He'd kill the baby!"

Gletha gave me a long look of disgust. "Frank won't kill no baby. Keep still and help me get them up."

I will never know how we managed. Pauline proved able to be helped to her feet. Gletha wrapped a cloth around her shoulders and one around mine. Together we floated through the moonlight. The wolves were still caroling in the distance. The scavenging deer watched us closely.

Across the field I saw my father outlined in the kitchen window of the shack, backed by the light from the kerosene lamp. As we reached the front steps, he threw open the door and shouted angrily at Gletha, "What are you doing here, witchlady? Trying to take my kid away from me again so he can roam the woods with you like some animal? You know you ain't welcome here!"

Gletha stepped aside to reveal Pauline with the baby in her arms. My daddy drew in a sharp breath, "Pauline Pucharski, what you got there?"

Pauline stepped forward—and placed her baby in my angry father's arms. His expression became tender.

He turned back into the house. We all followed. He stepped into the tiny living room. It was illumined only by light from the flames in the potbellied stove which danced through the isinglass panel and forested the wall with the shadow of the crooked little Christmas tree in the corner.

The tree had been the source of a terrible battle between my folks. As Dad carried it into the house, Mom exploded, "Frank! With all the beautiful, perfect trees in the woods, why did you have to cut that crooked, sickly-looking thing to celebrate Jesus' birthday?"

"Because, Mary, straight trees will grow into straight lumber which will come in handy if we ever decide someday to build a better house than we got. And it seems to me that Jesus can be served by the crooked as well as the straight."

He sat down in a wooden rocker, the lines of its back softened by a crocheted piece featuring a deer in mid-leap and a text reading, "God Bless Our Happy Home." He began rocking the baby. The chair creaked comfortably. Pauline, Gletha and I were momentarily mesmerized into a sense of well-being.

My mother came bustling in from their bedroom, completely engulfed in her long flannel nightgown. She immediately took charge. "Well, Pauline, at least we know what you've been doing the last few months! Frank, you just give me that baby right now. Gletha, you been real helpful, I'm sure. Now, why don't you just go home to Pud and have a real merry Christmas."

Gletha paused by the rocking chair. To my amazement, my daddy held the baby out to her. She blew on her index finger for a moment and made a star-shaped motion over the baby's forehead. She hugged Pauline and disappeared wordlessly into the night.

My mother swept the baby from my father's arms, saying, "Pauline, you just come right along with me. You and the baby can sleep in Roger's bed. You'll be real comfy under his new goosedown comforter. Why, you can sleep straight through tomorrow."

Forgetting Pauline and the season—and ordinary human decency—I exploded, "She's not going to sleep under my new goosedown comforter. It's my only present and I've been planning for months to sleep under it on Christmas Eve!"

Pauline looked at me. Her face was a sad mask of understanding and fatigue.

Mother spun on me. "I'm ashamed of you. They called you a little walking Bible that night at the church. You seem to have forgot the verse about it being more blessed to give than receive. You just git yourself to the kitchen. You can sleep on the floor out there by the warm stove under your old blankets which have been good enough for you for years."

She put an arm around Pauline. "Now, you two come on

in here and settle down. I don't want you to be any more ex-posed to complications than you been already."

I headed for the kitchen and a night on the hard, faded linoleum floor. Before turning in, I made one last trip to the outhouse. In the distance I saw Gletha, the goatlady, stand-ing in the midst of the gathered deer. Across the field came the grey shadows of the once-distant choristers. The deer seemed unafraid. As I returned, a momentary tableau of peace on earth glowed in the waning moon.

The next morning I was awakened by an unexpected sound—my daddy whistling! When he moved into one of his darknesses, it was usually at least two weeks before he could face the world with anything like joy. I realized that my mother and I must have both overslept. I attempted to un-tangle myself from the discomfort-tossed blankets when the kitchen door opened and Dad came in. To my surprise, he carried two pails of milk. He kicked me, though not as hard as usual. "Get up, you lazy kid. I got another Christmas pres-ent for you—I done your milking. Put it through the separator while I clean up. Then we'll take a little look at that baby."

My mother rushed in, trying to hide her unaccustomed lateness. "Frank, we are not going to disturb Pauline and the baby. They've had a long, hard night, and all of us need a little extra sleep once in a while. We'll have our breakfast, and then we'll see about our visitors."

While Dad splashed noisily at the sink, I poured the milk into the separator tank and turned the handle just the right speed so that the spinning disks would force the cream and the skim milk from their proper spouts. I thought again of Gletha seated in her kitchen the night before—and the carol's tune struck a proper rhythm for my task.

We sat down to a Yuletide breakfast of scrambled eggs, venison, cinnamon toast and special apple pie—the thumb-embossed crust riding the pan's edge and the outline of a Christmas tree pricked into the top crust where the steam escaped. Dad spoke only of the baby—how tiny and soft it was—how it just fit the curve of his arm—what a good lad it was not to cry all night.

Finally, he could wait no longer. The three of us tiptoed to my bedroom door and opened it carefully. Pauline Pucharski, the baby and my goosedown comforter were gone. They'd disappeared without a trace. My mother was flustered. Tears of disappointment glistened in my father's eyes. I was just plain mad: my only Christmas present stolen by somebody I always felt sort of close to.

I stormed into the living room. In the excitement of the morning, the fire had gone out. The scraggly tree was sitting on a bare, empty nail keg. It was decorated with the eleven scratched red balls and the worn tinsel.

I sat down on the cold floor and stared glumly at the presentless tree. Then, I saw it. Hanging from a lower branch, glistening in the Christmas morning sunlight, was the Polish opal.

That Christmas I had actually received four presents I could touch: a goosedown comforter, two pails of milk and a Polish opal. Down the years I have discovered two memory gifts to be cherished far beyond touch: the holy made human in a moonlit goatshed—and the brief, beautiful sound of my daddy whistling.

AUTHOR'S NOTE TO THE READER

My stories arise out of two central convictions: the sacred dwells at the heart of creation, the sacred dwells in the human heart. I live and write improvisationally as I attempt to recover that sacred sense which we in our freedom too often destroy around ourselves, in ourselves and in others.

My improvisations are disciplined by educational experiences, including a B.A. degree from Hamline University with an English/theater/religion emphasis, work in the Rockefeller Program of Religion and Theater at New York's Union Theological Seminary which combined with graduate study at Columbia University to culminate in a Master of Arts degree in English Dramatic Literature. A Master of Divinity degree from Oberlin Graduate School of Theology completed the formal prelude to lifelong improvisation.

Informally, the world of story was uniquely opened by three months of study with M'Butu, a black storyteller from South Africa. The stories in this volume rise on the wings of his spirit.

My sensitivities have been deepened by the richness of thirty-three years of marriage to Patricia Rothwell Robbennolt. Over thirty of those years have been spent not only as husband and wife but as co-pastors.

Our three children, Evelyn, Nicola and Grant—now scattered through their twenties—allowed me to spend hundreds of hours reading aloud to them from favorite storytellers. In the process I absorbed rhythms and images and sonorities which I unabashedly borrow in storytelling concerts and on the printed page.

Five Congregational Churches within the United Church of Christ have enhanced my exploration of the story-drama which explodes out of the heart of a caring God. These stories contain seeds sown by searching folk Patricia and I have

served in Stamford, Connecticut; Oberlin, Ohio; Tampa, Florida; Pasadena, California and Walla Walla, Washington.

A single theme sings through my stories: unexpected people/places of refuge are offered us. Within these centers of refuge healing happens, and we emerge renewed and more fully able to love ourselves and those around us who dwell in brokenness.

I wander the country telling these and other tales in concert halls, in churches, in university artist series and in public schools. I do workshops on the art of storytelling and lecture in college religion, psychology, English and education classes. As I improvise my way through these settings, my stories call forth a great deal of repressed pain in the listeners while at the same time lifting up possibilities for resolution and healing.

My children assure me that I no longer know where fact ends and fantasy begins. Dear children, you're absolutely right. However, if that line is ever re-drawn, the pain of my childhood will haunt me once again into despair, and the healing power of fantasy will be lost.

My hope is that this volume will be a creative place of refuge and healing.

Roz Rottennolt